BOILERPLATE

BOILERPLATE
★ HISTORY'S MECHANICAL MARVEL ★

PAUL GUINAN
—and—
ANINA BENNETT

ABRAMS IMAGE
NEW YORK

ACKNOWLEDGMENTS

The authors would like to acknowledge the following institutions and individuals,
who provided assistance in the researching of Boilerplate's saga.

The exceptional curators at the Campion Foundation allowed unprecedented access to their archives,
without which this book could not have been made. The Chicago History Museum, Smithsonian Institution,
and Library of Congress are resources that any history buff should visit.

Thanks to the generous Jonathan Case, Mike Friedrich, David Hahn, Jesse Hamm, Steve Lieber,
Mark Nuismer, David Oakes, Jeff Parker, Rich Powers, Eric Shanower, James Sinclair, and Susan Tardif.
Gratitude to Melanie Bell, Gordon Buffonge, Matthew Clark, Sean Guinan, and Denis Kitchen.
Special thanks to Terri Nelson, Bakers Mark, Collectors Press, David Cashion, and the dime-novel expertise
of Joe Rainone. Finally, a tip of the hat to the talented and gentlemanly Chris Elliott.

Editor: David Cashion
Designer: Think Studio, NYC
Production Manager: Jacqueline Poirier

Library of Congress Cataloging-in-Publication Data
Guinan, Paul.
Boilerplate : history's mechanical marvel /
by Paul Guinan and Anina Bennett.
p. cm.
ISBN 978-0-8109-8950-4
I. Bennett, Anina. II. Title.
PN6728.G769B65 2009
741.5'973—dc22
2008053763

Printed and bound in China
10 9 8 7 6 5 4 3 2 1

115 West 18th Street
New York, NY 10011
www.abramsbooks.com

FOREWORD *by* **SEAN G. DAVID**
PAGE 7

CHAPTER 1
PROFESSOR ARCHIBALD CAMPION: AN INVENTOR'S LIFE
- or -
THE BIRTH OF BOILERPLATE
PAGE 9

CHAPTER 2
WONDER OF THE WHITE CITY
- or -
THE MECHANICAL MAN MEETS THE PUBLIC
PAGE 21

CHAPTER 3
BOILERPLATE AT HOME AND ABROAD
- or -
AN AUTOMATON'S ADVENTURES
PAGE 33

CHAPTER 4
TALES OF A METAL DOUGHBOY
— or —
BOILERPLATE IN COMBAT
PAGE 67

CHAPTER 5
THE WAR TO END ALL WARS
- or -
BOILERPLATE'S FINAL BATTLE
PAGE 107

CHAPTER 6
POPULAR DEPICTIONS OF BOILERPLATE
- or -
THE ROBOT, REMEMBERED
PAGE 133

APPENDIX
BOILERPLATE'S BRETHREN
- or -
MECHANICAL MEN OF HISTORY
PAGE 149

TIME LINE
PAGE 158

BOILERPLATE TODAY
PAGE 162

INDEX
PAGE 164

FOREWORD

Prepare to meet the world's first robot soldier—not in a present-day military lab, or a futuristic science fiction movie, but in the past. Meet Boilerplate, the mechanical man invented by Professor Archibald Campion in 1893.

Designed as a prototype, for the self-proclaimed purpose of "*preventing the deaths of men in the conflicts of nations*," Professor Campion's Mechanical Marvel charged into combat alongside such notables as Teddy Roosevelt and Lawrence of Arabia. Campion and his robot also trekked to the South Pole, saved Pancho Villa's life, made silent movies, and hobnobbed with the likes of Mark Twain and Nikola Tesla.

Boilerplate is one of history's great enigmas, a technological breakthrough that languished in obscurity—until now. Ironically, the robot's fame in years past was part of the problem. Many researchers have been led astray by apocryphal tales of the automaton, and there's confusion about whether Boilerplate existed at all. As a result, historians are reluctant to include the robot in official texts.

I first discovered Boilerplate while researching an article about Gen. John "Black Jack" Pershing, who commanded the American Expeditionary Force during World War I. I kept running across tantalizing references to what seemed to be a mechanical soldier in original sources from throughout Pershing's career, starting in 1898.

Contemporary accounts offhandedly dismiss the robot's cognitive potential and personality. The prevailing view was that Boilerplate couldn't possibly possess noble human qualities such as courage and self-sacrifice. This reaction likely springs from generalized fears about the dawn of automation in the Victorian era, when machines were beginning to supplant human workers. To many writers of the time, Boilerplate was a paradox, representing both the pinnacle of human invention and a threat to that same inventive spirit.

To the pre–World War military, which wasn't yet accustomed to mechanized warfare, the notion of replacing the stalwart infantryman with a machine seemed dishonorable. Many people still thought of war as a valorous pursuit, in which men as well as nations distinguished themselves on the battlefield. Today, self-guided missiles and remote-controlled battle drones make the notion of an anthropomorphic robot soldier seem quaint.

I wonder: What would warfare look like today if we had built a robot army in 1917?

—Sean G. David, author of *History Repeats: Lessons from the Gilded Age*

CHAPTER 1

PROFESSOR ARCHIBALD CAMPION: AN INVENTOR'S LIFE

⎯⎯ or ⎯⎯

THE BIRTH OF BOILERPLATE

Boilerplate's inventor, Archibald Campion, was the youngest child of Robert and Jane Campion, who married in Washington, D.C., before the Civil War. Archie's older sister, Lily, was born there in 1852. The family's lives changed course at the first Battle of Bull Run in 1861, the famous engagement in which Confederate General "Stonewall" Jackson got his nickname.

Professor Archibald Balthazar Campion (1862–1938) and his greatest invention: Boilerplate. Chicago, November 1893.

PICNIC AT BULL RUN

The Campions were among a crowd of genteel civilians who turned out to picnic while watching the battle, expecting Jackson to be trounced. In those days, war was still occasionally a spectator sport, with a circumscribed field of battle. Jane, who had just learned that she was pregnant again, looked forward to sharing the news with her husband during their pleasant outing.

Archie and Lily's parents, Robert and Jane Campion, circa 1870.

↑ Archie's parents were among the many civilians who came from nearby Washington, D.C., to picnic and observe this historic engagement between North and South. They soon learned that war was no longer a formal affair.

↑ When Archie was a boy, he read some of the earliest science fiction dime novels. Pulp magazines such as this one helped inspire him to create Boilerplate.

➡ Artillery shot destroys a carriage directly in front of Robert and Jane Campion during the first Battle of Bull Run, July 21, 1861. They and other spectators fled toward Washington, D.C. as the Union army was unexpectedly driven back by Confederate forces.

It didn't work out that way. Instead, Union forces were beaten back by the rebels. Onlookers panicked and fled, their carriages clogging the roads back to D.C. Surrounded by explosions and gunfire, the Campions narrowly missed being hit by an artillery shot. Jane watched in horror as it blew apart one of her best friends nearby. As a result of the shock, she suffered a miscarriage.

Grieving and shaken by their close encounter with the gruesome reality of war, Robert and Jane decided to start over in a new town out west.

"ALL IS ASTIR HERE"

The Campions relocated to a city that teemed with possibilities: Chicago. They arrived during the most rapid urban expansion in human history. Between 1837 and 1871, Chicago exploded from a swampy outpost of 5,000 settlers to a bustling metropolis of 330,000 urbanites.

"Now, upon my return to Chicago after a mere three years abroad, I find myself absolutely astounded by its marvellous growth and improvement in that span. Foot by foot, inch by inch, Chicagoans have overtaken and transmuted swampland, clay-banks, and shifting sands. The city grows by day, by night, all days, unceasingly. In short, all is astir here."

—Patience Boyden, "New City on the Prairie," *The New York World* (March 25, 1871)

Born in Chicago on November 27, 1862, Archie Campion was an exceptionally curious child with a voracious appetite for knowledge. He learned to read at an early age, devouring dime novels called *Edisonades* that featured the adventures of inventors such as Johnny Brainerd and his steam-powered mechanical man.

As a young boy, Archie emulated his dime-novel hero, drawing diagrams and building clockwork toys. Later in life Archie would read about, and ultimately befriend, famous real-life inventors such as Frank Reade Jr. and Nikola Tesla.

A SLIGHT MISCALCULATION

Robert Campion tried to capitalize on the burgeoning business scene by founding the first company in Chicago to produce differential calculating machines. It was, however, an idea slightly ahead of its time, and Robert struggled to make a living from his business. Jane helped support their family by teaching history and writing adventure fiction under a pseudonym. She educated their children at home and often acted out her tall tales as bedtime stories, no doubt contributing to the dashing spirit Lily and Archie displayed throughout their lives.

Lily blossomed into a beautiful, whip-smart young lady with uncommon ideas—such as the notion that women should be allowed to vote and attend college. She met her match in an open-minded naval officer named Hugh W. McKee. The two wed in 1870, after a courtship during which Lily and Hugh grew deeply attached to each other, and Archie came to love Hugh as an older brother.

When Archie learned that Hugh was being sent to Korea, a strange land where the people didn't seem to like us very much,

he got worried. The Campions raised their son with no illusions about seeking glory in battle. Unlike many boys his age, he thought of war as deadly and cruel—something to be avoided if at all possible. Every day, he asked if there was news from his older brother-in-law.

Sadly, Archie's concern was justified: Hugh was killed in the brief Korean War of 1871. His death profoundly affected both Lily and Archie. It's little wonder that Archie turned his talents to inventing a mechanical substitute for human soldiers. His later declaration that he created Boilerplate "*for use in resolving the conflicts of nations without the deaths of men*" was directly inspired by Hugh's death.

Mere months after losing Hugh, tragedy struck Lily and Archie again: Their parents died in the Great Chicago Fire. Although their house survived, the siblings were left with little inheritance, and Lily's pension from the Navy was a pittance. To support herself and her young brother, Lily took up her mother's former work as a teacher and writer.

Lily Campion, Archie's sister. Her inner circle included actress Ethel Barrymore and First Daughter Alice Roosevelt.

Chicago in 1870, before the Great Fire.

THE FIRST KOREAN WAR

The Korean War of the 1950s wasn't the first time the United States did battle on Korean soil. In 1871, only six years after the American Civil War ended, the U.S. Navy sent armed forces to what Americans then called Corea. The ensuing conflict— the first Korean War—became the driving force behind Archie Campion's creation of Boilerplate.

GUNBOAT DIPLOMACY

Korea, the *Hermit Kingdom*, is strategically located between Japan and China. The United States, France, and Britain were all angling to open up Korea to foreign trade in 1853. But the

Korean monarchy had adopted an isolationist stance and wanted nothing to do with Western nations.

In spring 1871, American naval forces embarked for Korea, ostensibly to secure a treaty guaranteeing the safety of shipwrecked U.S. sailors. The expedition was headed by Rear Admiral John Rodgers, commander of the U.S. Asiatic Fleet. With him was Frederick Low, the American minister to China. They took along five ships, eighty-five cannon, and more than 1,200 men—including Lily Campion's husband, Lt. Hugh McKee. At the time, it was the largest American military force ever to land on foreign soil.

U.S. Marine Pvt. Hugh Purvis and Cpl. Charles Brown display a captured Korean battle flag during the first Korean War, June 1871. Both men were awarded the Medal of Honor for their actions in the American assault on Korean forts. With them is Capt. McLane Tilton, commanding marines, who reported that more than half of the ammunition supplied to the expedition was defective.

All photos of this conflict were taken by Felice Beato, the first war photojournalist. His career began in the mid-nineteenth century, when he photographed the Crimean War and the Sepoy Rebellion. By the time he joined the Corean Expedition in 1871, Beato was the most famous photographer on the planet.

"SOME SMALL DISQUIET"

"I hope the newspapers' dire predictions about the Corean Expedition have not alarmed you. Undeniably there are dangers: We have little knowledge of the people and the coastline, and to you, dearest Lily, I confess feeling some small disquiet when I weigh our numbers against ten millions of savages. Nevertheless, our mission is a peaceful one, and thus I do not think we shall have any trouble to speak of. You must tell Archie that we are all quite jolly at sea, and I forbid you both to fret or brood for my sake."
—Lt. Hugh McKee, letter to Lily Campion (May 17, 1871)

⬆ Lieutenant Hugh McKee (wearing the white cap), poses with his men aboard the stern of the USS *Colorado*. Only a few days after this photo was taken, McKee was killed while leading these men in an assault on a Korean fort.

➡ The USS *Colorado*, flagship of the Corean Expedition. This hybrid vessel, built in the transitional era that followed the great age of sail, was equipped to run on wind-powered sails as well as steam-driven propellers.

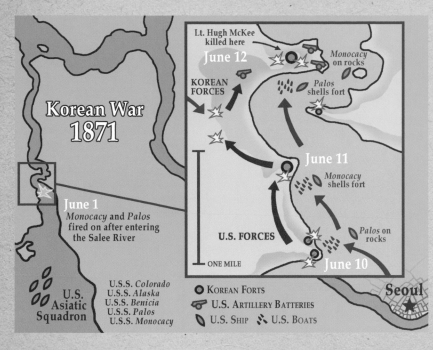

Korean War 1871

Lt. Hugh McKee killed here
June 12
KOREAN FORCES
Monocacy on rocks
Palos shells fort

June 11
Monocacy shells fort

June 1
Monocacy and *Palos* fired on after entering the Salee River

U.S. FORCES
ONE MILE

Palos on rocks
June 10

Seoul

U.S. Asiatic Squadron

U.S.S. *Colorado*
U.S.S. *Alaska*
U.S.S. *Benicia*
U.S.S. *Palos*
U.S.S. *Monocacy*

⊙ KOREAN FORTS
▮ U.S. ARTILLERY BATTERIES
◠ U.S. SHIP ✦ U.S. BOATS

Korean officials aboard the USS *Colorado* in 1871. The Koreans were strict isolationists, but their protocol during negotiations was to say nothing rather than directly refuse a request.

CULTURE WARS

Upon reaching Korea, the Americans anchored near the mouth of the Yomha River, which leads straight into the capital city of Seoul. They were greeted by polite but noncommittal Korean officials. Thanks to a near-total ignorance about Korean culture, Rodgers mistakenly thought the officials' lack of protest meant they agreed to his plan to send boats upriver toward the capital city of Seoul. But when U.S. vessels proceeded up the river, the Koreans fired on them.

← On the first day of the *Weekend War*, an amphibious force from the USS *Palos* struggles to bring ashore howitzers across a 200-yard mudflat. In the background, USS *Monocacy* fires on Choji Fortress.

↓ The USS *Monocacy*. Because of its shallow draft, this paddle-wheel steamer was chosen to go upriver on the punitive mission. It carried Lily Campion's husband, Hugh McKee, to his final battle.

On June 10, U.S. forces launched a punitive attack. Over the next three days, they torched forts and villages along the river, killing at least 350 Koreans. Hugh McKee was one of only three American fatalities, cut down during the final assault on the Korean fort that had fired the first volley. Three U.S. Navy ships have since been named USS *McKee* in his honor.

Having exacted revenge for what they perceived as Korean treachery, yet with no treaty in hand, Rodgers and Low departed less than a month later. In Korea, this short yet significant clash is remembered as *Shinmiyangyo*, or *Western Disturbance in the Shinmi Year*.

Ironically, the whole misadventure worked against the United States' underlying aim of opening Korea to Western trade. The Koreans considered themselves at war with America for the next ten years, and the region has been a political flash point for more than a century.

↑ The bodies of Korean defenders at Kwangsungbo Fortress, where Lt. Hugh McKee was killed. Captain McLane Tilton later wrote: "*Our mission to Corea has been a perfect failure.*"

UP IN FLAMES

During the same cruel year that young Archie lost his beloved brother-in-law in the Korean War, he lost his parents in the Great Chicago Fire. The conflagration raged for three terrible days: October 8–10, 1871. It consumed more than 2,000 acres, 18,000 buildings, and 300 lives. At least 100,000 Chicagoans were left homeless on the prairies. Even after the fire finally died out, the *Burned District* was literally too hot to deal with for days.

DON'T BLAME THE COW

At the same time, much bigger fires ravaged millions of acres across nearby states. One fire in Peshtigo, Wisconsin, killed at least 1,500 people and still ranks as the deadliest in U.S. his-

tory. Eyewitnesses in different locales reported spontaneous combustion and *"great balls of fire"* or *"fire balloons"* hurtling from the sky. Entire islands were burning in Lake Michigan.

Firefighters said that the blazes all started at multiple sites during the same twenty-four-hour period, they were all infernally hot, and they all

⬆ The pattern formed by simultaneous fires across the Midwest correlates with the distribution of fragments of Biela's Comet after its disintegration.

quickly flared out of control. They were probably touched off by meteorite fragments of Biela's Comet, which used to cross Earth's orbit every 6.6 years. The comet broke into large pieces sometime around 1846, appeared in 1852, and was later replaced by a series of meteor showers.

The Chicago Fire wasn't the biggest of the bunch, but it was the most heavily publicized, capturing the public imagination. The myth that it was started by Mrs. O'Leary's cow persists to this day, even though a *Chicago Tribune* reporter confessed to making up the cow story.

OUT OF THE ASHES

The swift recovery effort in Chicago immediately became a potent symbol of industry and urbanization. Legend has it that on the very same day that the last burning building was extinguished, the first load of lumber for rebuilding was delivered to Chicago.

Debris from the Burned District was shoved into Lake Michigan as landfill, expanding the size of downtown, and new buildings were erected atop the charred remnants of the old. Like the World's Columbian Exposition, the Great Chicago Fire marks the end of one era and the birth of another.

FROM ODD JOBS TO RICHES

After Lily and Archie were orphaned, Archie pitched in to support them during his teen years. He held a succession of positions that earned him money as well as technical experience. One of his favorite jobs was working as an operator for the Chicago Telephone Company during the late 1870s. He and his fellow operators—all boys during that period—were dubbed *wild Indians* at the company because of their rowdy behavior.

Youthful antics aside, Archie worked hard both on and off the clock, educating himself and conducting experiments at home. His scientific talents and dedication paid off. In 1882, he filed several patent applications for valvular conduits and polyphase electric systems. Within four years, Archie was a millionaire with guaranteed patent royalties for life from the Westinghouse Electric

& Manufacturing Company. He and Lily moved into a mansion on Chicago's posh Prairie Avenue.

Archie on the job at the Chicago Telephone Company in 1878, standing next to his supervisor's desk. In the background is an early telephone switchboard.

In 1886, though, Archie abruptly stopped filing patents and became reclusive. About two years later, he built a small laboratory in Chicago and began work on a mysterious project.

Archie Campion in his late twenties, when royalties from his first wave of patent licenses made him a millionaire.

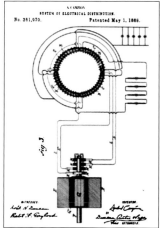

One of Archie's patent drawings, *System of Electrical Distribution*, 1886. Archie used the proceeds from his early patent licenses to finance the development and construction of Boilerplate. This one was issued shortly before Archie went into seclusion to create his mechanical marvel.

↑↑ Archie Campion built a small laboratory in the late 1880s specifically for his Boilerplate project, at the northwest corner of Wrightwood and Wilton on Chicago's north side. Two electric cars are parked in front of the lab: a Columbia Electric Dos-a-Dos Mark VI and, behind it, a Maxim Mark III. These automobiles and the elevated train tracks date this picture to sometime between 1897 and 1899.

↑ The building Boilerplate was born in still exists today. After Archie's death in 1938, the structure remained vacant until 1942, when it was converted into a factory to produce spare parts for airplanes during World War II. It later housed a succession of small-scale manufacturing companies. In the 1990s it was gutted, given a third floor, and refurbished as upscale residential lofts.

SECRET SCIENCE

The ever-inventive Archie designed his own lab equipment. He incorporated devices created by Edward Fullerton, pioneer of fuel-cell technology; Frank Reade Jr., creator of the Electric Man; and Nikola Tesla, genius of electromagnetics. Unfortunately, because most of Archie's notes and unique gear were later destroyed, they're lost to history.

Likewise, the technical details of Boilerplate's inner workings are a mystery today. We know only the broad strokes: Boilerplate was powered by customized Fullerton hydrogen fuel cells, its movements were stabilized by gyroscopes, and its electrical "nervous system" was based on Tesla's designs. Archie collaborated closely with Tesla and Fullerton while developing Boilerplate.

This allegorical image shows Archie Campion inviting Nikola Tesla (holding an electrical cord) and Edward Fullerton (holding a component of his fuel cell) to contribute to the creation of Boilerplate.

⬆ Boilerplate in the laboratory where it was created, 1894. The equipment seen here was constructed by Archie Campion, Edward Fullerton, and Nikola Tesla.

⬇ These are among the few surviving records of calculations made by Archie and Fullerton. Together the two scientists developed a new form of motive power for the mechanical man, *"based on neither steam nor electricity!"*

⬆ Archie's friend and colleague Edward Fullerton developed the first practical hydrogen fuel cell, then spent the rest of his career refining and testing various applications for his invention. Fullerton's fuel cells provided a compact, portable, renewable power source for Boilerplate, eliminating the need to haul around coal or batteries.

After his technology was used to propel boats on the lagoons of the 1893 World's Columbian Exposition—and a certain robot on display at Machinery Hall— in Chicago, the U.S. Navy kept Fullerton exclusively engaged.

The Navy also kept much of Fullerton's work under wraps. As a result, historians tend to view him as a scientific one-hit wonder, and he is even more obscure than Archie.

Fullerton and Archie collaborated on only one other scientific project: retrofitting the engines of the USS *Illinois* with a Fullerton power plant, during the world tour of the Great White Fleet in 1908.

⬆ Archie's fiftieth birthday, November 27, 1912. This is the only known photo of all three of the men who built Boilerplate. From left to right:

Edward Fullerton, who adapted his innovative fuel cells to serve as Boilerplate's power source

Frank Reade III, pioneering aeronaut and son of Archie's friend Frank Reade, Jr.

Archie Campion, father of modern robotics

Nikola Tesla, inventor of the AC electrical system and the first patented radio apparatus

NIKOLA TESLA
1856–1943

Thomas Edison usually gets credit for launching the Age of Electricity. But in fact, the father of our electronic world is a Serbian immigrant named Nikola Tesla.

The prolific Tesla laid the groundwork for our entire electrical grid—he invented the alternating-current (AC) generator, transformers, just about everything that makes it possible to transmit electricity over long distances—as well as radio, remote-controlled robotics, loudspeakers, fluorescent lights, hydroelectric generators, wireless power and data transmission, and countless other innovations that are still in use. He held more than 700 patents, and he made strikingly accurate predictions about the future. And he helped Archie Campion build Boilerplate.

Archie met Tesla while visiting New York in 1886, during the brief existence of the Tesla Electric Light and Manufacturing Company. These two geniuses relished one another's company, brainstorming and collaborating at every opportunity. They even shared a distaste for warfare, but Tesla's solutions differed from Archie's: Tesla dreamt of using technology to eradicate the underlying causes of war.

"Only through annihilation of distance in every respect, such as the conveyance of intelligence, transport of passengers and supplies, and transmission of energy, will conditions be brought about some day insuring permanency of friendly relations. What we now want most is closer contact and better understanding between individuals and communities all over the Earth, and the elimination of that fanatic devotion to exalted ideals of national egoism and pride which is always prone to plunge the world into primeval barbarism and strife."

—Nikola Tesla, "My Inventions: An Autobiography," *Electrical Experimenter* (1919)

Tesla's reputation as an eccentric eventually overshadowed his genius. His potential scientific legacy was diminished by the fact that, after his death, the FBI and the Office of Alien Property seized Tesla's papers and equipment. Many of Archie Campion's letters to Tesla never reappeared.

Nikola Tesla died on January 7, 1943, in New York City. A few months later, the U.S. Supreme Court at last declared that Tesla had patented the radio before Guglielmo Marconi did. But, like Edison, Marconi still gets all the credit.

"What a shame that circumstance prevented you from being present when the fruit of our long labors ripened! There was an awful moment when I feared all would come to naught.

"This past fortnight I endured nightmares, so vivid and affecting that I could scarce distinguish them from waking experience, of debacle in every form—from enormous electrical explosions to the silence of a stillborn machine. Were it not for the aid and comfort of our colleague

so enthused last week? I discovered it in the kitchen and presumed you might have need of it.'

"Scattered as I am, I had neglected to replace the Mark I power distributor with the misplaced Mark II. Immediately I rectified the oversight, and Fullerton and I resumed our stations. Ceremoniously we closed the circuit. At first there was another moment of awful silence, then an almost imperceptible buzzing, and then . . . my mechanical man's electrical 'eyes' alit from within, and it took its first step forward."

—Archibald Campion, letter to Nikola Tesla (April 13, 1893)

MEET ME AT THE FAIR

Between 1888 and 1891, there are no known published mentions of Archie. Then he resurfaced, reportedly with a new invention. But he refused to discuss it, other than to say that the curious-minded could come see for themselves at Machinery Hall during the most eagerly anticipated event of modern times: the 1893 World's Columbian Exposition.

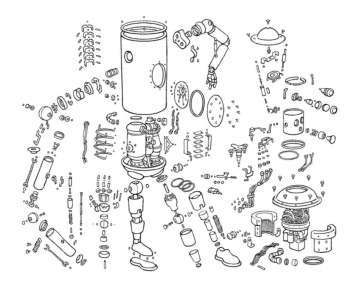

A partial exploded diagram of Boilerplate, extrapolated from the American First Army's WWI maintenance records.

Fullerton and my dear sister, Lily, I may well have fallen victim to my dreams, believing the experiment failed before it had truly begun.

"In fact, Lily once again demonstrated the inestimable value to science of common sense exercised by a discerning mind. At half-past eleven of this morning, Fullerton and I, having made every possible preparation, having thrice inspected every connection and gauge, stood at opposite poles of my laboratory and completed the circuit that should have activated my automaton. The result was nothing—not the slightest sound or movement.

"You may well imagine my despair. Like a madman I scuttled about, brushing aside poor Fullerton's proffered assistance, in vain seeking the fatal error. I was at my wits' end when Lily, who had come to investigate the cause of the commotion, happily conveyed with her its solution: 'Archie,' she said, 'is this not the device about which you and Mister Tesla were

The Inter Ocean.

CHICAGO DAY EDITION.

OCTOBER 9TH 1893.

C.W. SAALBURG

CHAPTER 2

WONDER OF THE WHITE CITY

or

THE MECHANICAL MAN MEETS THE PUBLIC

Archibald Campion was true to his word. In summer 1893, he revealed his latest creation: a walking, talking mechanical man. A robot.

A local newspaper takes pride in Chicago's rise from the ashes of the Great Conflagration to become a world-class urban center and host of the pinnacle of cultural achievement: an international exposition.

"UNFOLDED GENIUS"

Archie introduced Professor Campion's Mechanical Marvel—which didn't come to be known as *Boilerplate* until years later—at the World's Columbian Exposition, an ambitious world's fair held in Chicago.

The World's Columbian Exposition occupies a crucial juncture in U.S. history. It both reflected and shaped our nation's evolution, symbolizing as well as spurring the transition from agricultural to industrial, rural to urban, producer to consumer society. For Americans and Chicagoans alike, the 1893 World's Fair embodied aspirations to be seen in a new light, to play a more sophisticated role. For Archie Campion, it was the beginning of a new chapter in his life.

"So accustomed had I grown to working day in and day out, utterly absorbed in constructing my mechanical soldier, that upon its completion I felt at first a sense of great relief and accomplishment, followed at once by panic. Having created this

"MAKE NO LITTLE PLANS; THEY HAVE NO MAGIC TO STIR MEN'S BLOOD."
—Daniel H. Burnham, Director of Works, Columbian Exposition

marvel, I now face the far more onerous chore of peddling it like a street vendor!"

—Archibald Campion, letter to Mark Twain (May 1, 1893)

Archie was granted a space in Machinery Hall, one of the fourteen Great Buildings that housed most of the fair's 65,000 exhibits. Artfully landscaped canals, lagoons, and causeways connected these classically styled white edifices into an idealized, orderly *White City*. Electric boats plied the waters, powered by Edward Fullerton's fuel cells.

Inside Machinery Hall, Archie's exhibit was dwarfed by endless rows of state-of-the-art mechanical devices and tools, with special attractions such as Eli Whitney's cotton gin, the world's largest conveyor belt, and a cutting-edge power plant that generated electricity for the whole fair. At night the fairgrounds were illuminated by electric lights, thanks to an early alternating-current system developed by Archie's friend Nikola Tesla. The world had never seen anything like it.

"In the mammoth corridors of Machinery Hall at the World's Fair the zenith of nine-teenth century progress in the mechanical arts was reached, and the artisans of every civilized clime learned something of practical benefit from the unfolded genius of the world's great-est inventors. Perhaps most highly regarded by fellow inventors was Professor Campion's re-markable anthropomorphic machine, which imagination allows could be of varied benefit to mankind."

—Henry Davenport Northrop, *Pictorial History of the World's Fair* (Union Publishing House, 1893)

THE SOUNDS OF PROGRESS

Boilerplate's unveiling on May 23, 1893, less than two weeks after the fair opened, was a bit anticlimactic. Archie demonstrated the robot in front of a modest crowd, eliciting a few gasps.

"Cam and I visited Machinery Hall today... you recall how he does like to know about every newfangled thingamajig under the sun. Well, for once even he was confounded. There was this fellow called Champion, showing a kind of metal soldier. A big iron man.

It took two years and $25 million to transform 630 acres of swampy Chicago lakeshore into the neoclas-sical fantasyland of the 1893 World's Columbian Exposition. The guiding lights were Frederick Law Olmsted, who designed Central Park in Manhattan, and Daniel Burnham, who became a major force in architecture and urban planning. Burnham oversaw all the construc-tion, paying particular attention to the fair's fourteen Great Buildings, which collectively boasted 63 million square feet of floor space.

Originally intended to celebrate the 400th anniversary of Columbus's 1492 landing in North America, the fair was a bit late—but no one seemed to mind. It attracted around 27 million visitors, at a time when the population of the entire United States was only about 63 million. People even paid to gawk while it was under construction.

PROFESSOR CAMPION'S
MECHANICAL MARVEL

⬆ A rare interior view of Machinery Hall. Boilerplate peers down on Archie Campion's booth from the balcony. Some of the exhibit halls inside the Great Buildings, although copiously described in writing by various authors, were not well documented photographically.

➡ A souvenir postcard of Machinery Hall, one of the fair's fourteen Great Buildings and the site of Boilerplate's unveiling.

From the roof of the Manufactures and Liberal Arts Building, Boilerplate, Lily Campion, and a couple of Columbian Guards gaze southeast across the White City. Machinery Hall, where Boilerplate made its public debut, can be seen at upper right.

PROFESSOR CAMPION AND HIS METAL MANSERVANT

Dancing Girl
Street
of Cairo.

"*I tell you what, that contraption walked and talked all on its own! It lifted up two grown men over its head as if they was feathers. It saluted and marched about and aimed a rifle like a real soldier. They showed how it couldn't be hurt. At the end it looked square at me, bowed just as proper as you please, and said 'Good day ma-dam. Did you en-joy the de-mon-stra-tion?' 'I surely did' says I 'but I don't know why I'm telling that to a machine!' To which it says 'Be-cause I asked.'*"

—Jolene Gibson, letter to Susan Gibson (May 23, 1893)

Archie gave a short speech about the robot's intended purpose, which the audience greeted with polite applause before moving along to the next attraction. Due to the overwhelming noise from the multitude of machines being demonstrated in Machinery Hall, most spectators probably couldn't even hear what Archie had said.

"*I did not anticipate, and you may not be aware of, the deafening array of sounds emitted by the mechanical exhibits in Machinery Hall. This fact is conspicuously omitted from the many guidebooks, magazines, and pamphlets devoted to the Columbian Exposition. Imagine a single cavernous room, surpassing 435,000 square feet in floor area, filled with the unceasing din of banging, clanging, clattering, sparking, sputtering, squealing, hissing, and occasionally explosive devices, and you may have some inkling of what we endure. I am thankful that my aural capacity and Lily's do not seem to have suffered any ill effect.*"

—Archibald Campion, letter to Frank Reade Jr. (May 26, 1893)

Archie Campion tours the Midway Plaisance with his sister, Lily. She is being pushed along by Boilerplate in a rolling chair, a convenience available for rent at the fair (75 cents per hour or six dollars per day). The multiculturalism of the world's first Midway was a rarity in 1893. It was so full of strange sights that Boilerplate barely got a second glance from the crowds of curiosity seekers, most of whom were more interested in the Egyptian belly dancers.

➡ Boilerplate with its original military kit, which the robot wore during the Spanish-American War. At Winston Churchill's urging, the shoulder pouch and helmet designs were later adapted as part of the British Army's official field uniform.

⬅ Sketch artists experienced a surge in demand from a variety of magazines and special publications that commissioned illustrations to give their readers an inside view of the World's Columbian Exposition.

BAD TIMING

Although some of Archie's colleagues recognized the promise of the technology behind Boilerplate, the robot wasn't exactly an overnight sensation. On top of the noise problem in Machinery Hall, Archie was plagued by timing problems. For starters, the date he picked to unveil Boilerplate was the same day Thomas Edison chose to demonstrate the much-hyped *kinetoscope*, the forerunner of modern movie projectors, in the Electricity Building. It was most people's first chance to see the kinetoscope in action, and there was no resisting the siren call of a new form of entertainment.

Unlike most other exhibits, Boilerplate wasn't confined to its exhibit hall. Archie and Lily took the robot with them whenever they explored the fair. Their excursions generated enough public excitement that Archie *(cont. on page 28)*

THE WOMAN QUESTION

In the nineteenth century, women weren't allowed to vote, and there was still vigorous debate about whether they should even attend college or pursue careers. Early feminism was among

Susan B. Anthony speaks at the World's Congress of Representative Women. To the right of the lectern is Lily Campion, and behind her is Boilerplate.

the many modern issues aired at the World's Columbian Exposition. And Archie's sister, Lily Campion (1852–1952), was among those who played a part in staging the fair. She helped organize the World's Congress of Representative Women (WCW), a gathering of 500 female delegates representing twenty-seven countries and 126 organizations. Attendees included the illustrious Susan B. Anthony and Elizabeth Cady Stanton.

Bertha Honoré Palmer, wife of real estate and hotel magnate Potter Palmer, invited Lily to join the Board of Lady Managers for the Columbian Exposition. The Board was also responsible for the WCW and Woman's Building, a major exhibit hall showcasing the varied accomplishments of women from around the globe.

Lily Campion, 1900.

Boston architect Sophia Hayden, the first woman to earn a degree in architecture from MIT, designed it.

During the WCW, Lily formed close friendships with two fellow suffragists who would broaden her horizons considerably: Ida B. Wells, already renowned for her fiery antilynching activism, and social reformer Jane Addams.

"It requires philosophy and heroism to rise above the opinion of the wise men of all nations and races."
—Elizabeth Cady Stanton

ACROSS COLOR LINES

Ida B. Wells, the daughter of freed slaves, ran a newspaper in Memphis before coming to Chicago. She protested the paucity of African-American representation in the exhibit halls and the employment rolls of the World's Columbian Exposition. With Frederick Douglass, who represented Haiti at the fair, Wells wrote and distributed a pamphlet titled "The Reason Why the Colored American Is Not in the World's Columbian Exhibition."

"One had better die fighting against injustice than die like a dog or a rat in a trap."
—Ida B. Wells-Barnett

Lily's first encounter with her was not entirely friendly. Lily tried to convince Wells that she should give up her racial protest because it was divisive, and that women should present a united front. Wells told Lily that she ought to try living as a negro woman for a week and see if it changed her mind about "universal" women's issues. Once they calmed down enough to listen to each other, mutual respect began to emerge. From Wells, Lily learned to consider the priorities of African-American and proletarian suffragists—and got a new perspective on Boilerplate.

"Your brother's ill-conceived experiment is no better than slavery. If a mechanical man can walk and talk, is he not a man?"
—Ida B. Wells, letter to Lily Campion (October 26, 1893)

"OUR COMMON LIFE"

Jane Addams, who would become Lily's close friend and mentor, dedicated her life to peace and social justice—especially to improving the terrible living and working conditions of the urban poor. In 1889, she opened Hull House in a downtrodden industrial neighborhood of Chicago. Hull House offered free education, day care, an employment bureau, a public kitchen, library, art gallery, gymnasium, and more. It exists today as a museum.

During the WCW, Lily invited Addams to meet Boilerplate one-on-one. Addams was impressed, but she viewed

"The good we secure for ourselves is precarious and uncertain until it is secured for all of us and incorporated into our common life."
—Jane Addams

Archie's plan to put mechanical soldiers on the battlefield as a misguided effort that would only encourage warfare. Instead, she envisioned using Boilerplate to transform the urban wastelands in which she worked.

"There is stark contrast between the gleaming, artificial, attentively managed White City and the willfully neglected pockets of decay that fester in the real Chicago. In the area where Hull House is situated the streets are inexpressibly dirty, the number of schools inadequate, factory legislation unenforced, and the stables defy all laws of sanitation. Hundreds of houses are unconnected with the street sewer.

"Such wretched decay is needless even without technological aid. But it is inexcusable if we consider that all could be made right by such an innovation as mechanical maintenance men—all the crumbling quarters improved, the filthy dross removed, without human toil or injury."
—Jane Addams, "The Objective Value of a Social Settlement" (1893)

Lily and Archie continued to lobby for women's suffrage until the Nineteenth Amendment was finally passed in 1920. Then they worked to change discriminatory practices, such as poll taxes, that effectively prevented blacks from voting in many states. Their early efforts helped pave the way for the Voting Rights Act of 1965, although neither Archie nor Lily lived to see its passage.

WORLD'S FAIR FIRSTS

In the late nineteenth century, news still traveled slowly, if at all. The World's Columbian Exposition was a rare chance to experience technological progress, foreign cultures, art, amusements, and commerce all at once. People journeyed from all over the world to see it, and those who couldn't make the trip in person visited vicariously through illustrated books and periodicals.

It was simultaneously the best and the worst place to introduce an invention as innovative as Boilerplate. Below are just a few of the many other firsts vying for visitors' fragmented attention.

★ The Columbian Exposition was the first electrically powered fair in history. On its opening night of May 1, 1893, President Grover Cleveland pushed a button to light up the fairgrounds with 100,000 electric lamps.

★ Fairgoers rode the Intramural Railway, the first elevated electric railway. It was powered by a 2,000-horsepower engine with a shaft weighing sixty tons.

★ Americans got their first taste of Japanese culture on the fair's Wooded Island, a living village that included Japanese craftsmen, musicians, and actors.

★ Elisha Gray debuted the first fax machine: the telautograph, a device that electrically transmitted handwriting over long distances. "What you write in Chicago is instantly reproduced here in fac-simile."

★ Manufacturers launched new brands and foods that are still famous today:

> HAMBURGERS	> CRACKER JACKS
> DIET CARBONATED SODA	> CREAM OF WHEAT
> JUICY FRUIT GUM	> AUNT JEMIMA SYRUP
> PABST BEER	> SHREDDED WHEAT

★ The U.S. Postal Service produced its first picture postcards and commemorative stamp set, and the U.S. Mint offered its first commemorative coins.

★ Spray-painting was first used, to paint the interiors of the vast exhibit halls.

★ The amusement park was born, in the form of the Midway Plaisance: a wild collection of carnival rides, games, sideshows, snacks, and other concessions.

★ The popular Street in Cairo exhibit introduced belly dancing to America.

★ Young Harry Houdini and Scott Joplin, each still developing his respective art, performed on the Midway.

★ George W. Ferris built the first Ferris Wheel, a massive 250-foot-high steel structure with thirty-six cars, each the size of a bus.

The fair had a ripple effect on American design, art, manufacturing, literature, and just about everything else. When Henry Ford visited, for example, he saw an internal combustion engine that fueled his dreams of a horseless carriage. In the literary world, L. Frank Baum's Emerald City of Oz was based on the White City—and the Tin Man was inspired by none other than Boilerplate.

A souvenir spoon from the 1893 world's fair. Embossed on the handle is an image of Boilerplate's head, and on the bowl is Machinery Hall.

decided to invite the press to a pre-scheduled Boilerplate publicity tour of the fairgrounds.

But that went awry, too: They were upstaged by the Infanta (Princess) Eulalia of Spain, the youngest daughter of Queen Isabella II. Eulalia, visiting as an official representative of her country, was greeted with much pomp and circumstance. Royalty had become chic again in the United States, and all eyes were on the Infanta wherever she went. Boilerplate garnered only a smattering of press coverage, mainly as a curiosity.

"It was my fine fortune to be present when the mechanical man and its inventor perambulated the Fair grounds. Everywhere, they were the objects of astonished glances, exclamations of wonder, and the occasional shriek from a timid soul. I scarcely believed my own ears when the automaton uttered a direct reply to my query about its activities: 'I will ride in the Ferris Wheel.' That leg of its tour attracted a considerable number of onlookers, all of whom were, alas, entirely excluded from hobnobbing with the machine-man owing to its being so heavy as to require a private car on the great Wheel."

—Nicholas Stanley Parker, "The Walking Mechanical Miracle of the World's Fair," *World's Columbian Exposition Extra* (June 1893)

Boilerplate was not, in fact, heavy enough to warrant its own car on the Ferris Wheel. Each car was the size of a bus and could hold sixty people. A more likely explanation is that the robot's weight was used as an excuse, in order to avoid any disputes over who would get to ride in the same car with it.

Even Archie's announced purpose for Boilerplate, as a prototype soldier *"for use in resolving the conflicts of nations,"* wasn't particularly well timed. Despite growing social unrest and economic disparity within its borders, the U.S. was officially at peace with other nations in 1893.

Most people had never heard of the 1871 Korean War, and of course no one yet knew that in only five years the United States would invade Cuba and the Philippines during the Spanish-American War. Or that the next century would bring two unthinkable world wars. The idea of a mechanical soldier was easily shrugged off as fanciful and unnecessary.

INFORMATION OVERLOAD

In retrospect, it's hard to understand how such an advanced, groundbreaking invention as Boilerplate could have gotten lost in the shuffle. But at the time, there were so many special events and celebrities, so many novelties and exotic cultures being introduced to a dazzled public, that a man-size automaton seemed only mildly remarkable. There was too much competition.

The fair showcased *"every device that genius could suggest and money supply,"* in the words of Bertha Honoré Palmer, who headed the Board of Lady Managers. Exhibitors from around the globe brought with them all manner of inventions, materials, goods, arts, foodstuffs, machinery, ideas, publications, crafts, games, and customs. Back then, it was the closest thing to a collective, interactive knowledge base like the Internet—but in physical form, all in one place, and temporary.

To average fairgoers, Boilerplate was certainly a sight to see, yet merely one of countless clever innovations. Many people were delighted in equal measure by the robot, the world's first Ferris Wheel, and the convenient new hot cereal mix called *Cream of Wheat*.

"The World's Fair of 1893 was an astounding, bewildering assemblage of art and industry, all the more so for a young lad still in short pants. Matthew recalls: 'I saw so many wonderful

This embroidered ribbon, handed out at the fair as a souvenir in Machinery Hall, is now a rare collectible.

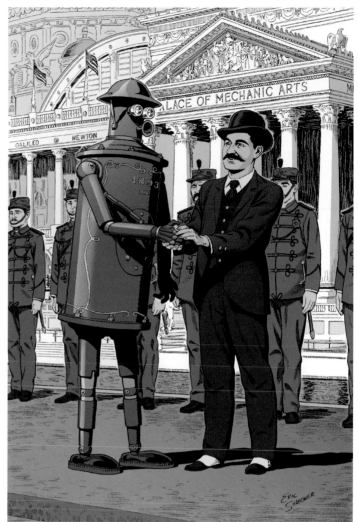

The Tin Man undergoes repair. William Wallace Denslow, the original *Oz* artist, patterned the look of the Tin Man after Boilerplate at Baum's request.

things that I hardly knew what I liked most, and it all is so confused in my mind that I hardly know now what I did see.

"'Two things I recollect of note, one being my first glimpse of an electrified city at night, the Court of Honor lighted as though by stars come down from the heavens. The other being the brief terror of accidental parting from my parents, then the thrill of getting whisked up by Professor Campion's metal man, what found my family and reunited us. How my brother was the picture of envy! He tried to keep me from viewing the Monster Cheese in the Agricultural Building, but Mum and Dad wouldn't have none of his fuss.'"

—Edith Aldrich, interview with Matthew McKeough, *Memories of the White City* (Pericles Press, 1909)

SHADOW ON THE WHITE CITY

Boilerplate and other lesser-known exhibits were also overshadowed in the public mind by a series of tragedies surrounding the World's Columbian Exposition, including several fires, a smallpox epidemic, and the assassination of Chicago's Mayor Carter Harrison the day before the fair closed.

"Poor Archie. He certainly had not expected instantaneous success, nor was personal notoriety his objective. He desired only to spread word of his invention and foster interest in its potential military and commercial applications. The obstacles fate has thus far placed in his path are comically multitudinous. The fair, it seems, was precisely the wrong venue for the debut of his automatic soldier. We have discovered a new irony of the modern age: In a place where every thing is a wonderment, nothing is a wonderment."

—Lily Campion, letter to Paula Vincent (November 27, 1893)

Archie and Lily persevered, hatching a plan to show off Boilerplate's strength and versatility on an expedition to the South Pole. But while they laid their plans, Boilerplate would be drawn into its first armed conflict—on the streets of Chicago.

A NEW AGE

The United States hadn't yet become a world power in 1893, but the country was obviously entering a new era. The closing of the American frontier came to represent the demarcation between past and future. The end of our westward expansion was announced at

Buffalo Bill's Wild West Show performed just outside the Columbian Exposition as historian Frederick Jackson Turner declared that the United States' western frontier was closed, its pioneer days over.

the Columbian Exposition, in a milestone speech by historian Frederick Jackson Turner. As he spoke, Buffalo Bill was staging a Wild West side show next door to the fair. With the geographic frontier vanishing, its familiar elements—cowboys and Indians, covered wagons and Winchesters—were transformed into nostalgic icons. At the same time, Boilerplate and other technological marvels were being introduced, opening up new frontiers in science and industry.

"What the Mediterranean Sea was to the Greeks, breaking the bond of custom, offering new experiences, calling out new institutions and activities, that, and more, the ever retreating frontier has been to the United States directly, and to the nations of Europe more remotely. And now, four centuries from the discovery of America, at the end of a hundred years of life under the Constitution, the frontier has gone, and with its going has closed the first period of American history."

—Frederick Jackson Turner, "The Significance of the Frontier in American History" (1893)

THE PANIC OF 1893

Unfortunately, the transition to the industrial era was rough. During the late 1800s, known as the *Gilded Age*, a new class of wealthy business owners or *robber barons* came to power. Their fortunes were built on uncontrolled industrial growth, urbanization, and mass immigration that provided cheap labor. The flip side was economic crashes, violent labor clashes, and mass poverty. Erstwhile farmers struggled to adjust to dangerous factory work and commercialized city life, while the emerging business elite raked in profits.

In 1893, despite the promise and fanfare of the Columbian Exposition—and politicians who continued to insist that the American economy was healthy—the country was teetering on the brink of a severe depression. The collapse of several major U.S. railroads pushed it over the edge, touching off a financial panic. An estimated 500 banks and 16,000 businesses went under during the 1890s. At the depression's low point, about two out of every ten people were jobless. This type of cycle would be repeated in later years, most recently in the Great Financial Crisis that began in 2008.

Because there was no unemployment insurance, Social Security, or employee benefits of any kind in 1893, many citizens had nowhere to turn for help. Their desperate responses ranged from suicide to a mass march of the unemployed, dubbed *Coxey's Army*, on Washington, D.C. Jack London, who would later cross paths with Boilerplate at least twice and go on to become a famous author, marched with Coxey's Army as a teen.

But the death throes of the Gilded Age were also the birth pangs of populism and the Progressive Era. Many rights and protections that we take for granted now, such as child labor laws, food safety regulation, women's right to vote, and national parks, were first established during the Progressive Era in the early twentieth century.

Archie Campion, through luck and foresight, managed to weather the Panic of 1893 and other large-scale economic crises with his personal wealth intact. Millions of other Americans weren't so fortunate.

During the Gilded Age, many of the rich genuinely feared that the poor would rise up against them. Yet the nation's business leaders resisted legislative attempts to remedy the dramatic social inequities of the day, instead using armed force to quell unrest.

The bustling corner of Dearborn and Randolph in downtown Chicago, 1909. Note the preponderance of streetcars. After World War II, a group of corporations—including General Motors, Firestone, and Standard Oil—bought up electric streetcar companies in cities throughout the U.S., then dismantled the systems and replaced them with gasoline-powered buses.

↑ The first national march on Washington, D.C., occurred in spring 1894, during a terrible depression. Led by Jacob Coxey, *Coxey's Army* petitioned the government to create working-class jobs. Frank L. Baum's *The Wizard of Oz* refers to this event allegorically: A Scarecrow (farmer), Tin Woodman (factory worker), and Cowardly Lion (politician) march to the Emerald City (capital), asking for redress from the Wizard (President).

← The Great Panic of 1893 was the worst economic crisis the United States had ever seen. Even middle-class families were reduced to waiting in line for meals at charity kitchens. The inset panel shows a Chicago cop keeping watch on homeless people who took shelter in City Hall.

At the time, there was little to no regulation of financial markets and corporations, and no public aid. As a result, when stocks crashed and businesses collapsed, millions of people lost their jobs, their homes, and even their lives.

CHAPTER 3

BOILERPLATE
AT HOME AND ABROAD

—~— *or* —~—

AN AUTOMATON'S ADVENTURES

In 1894, while the United States was mired in a deep financial depression, Boilerplate took part in a dramatic labor dispute that opened Archie Campion's eyes to the hardships faced by working-class people.

Poster for the 1899 theatrical adaptation of Jack London's Boilerplate serial.

THE PERFECT TOWN

It occurred fourteen miles south of downtown Chicago, where manufacturing tycoon George Pullman had built a perfect little town for his workers and their families. The town contained perfect little rowhouses, a church, a library, shops, and a theater. George was so pleased that he named the town after himself: Pullman. At the nearby Pullman Palace Car Company plant, his workers made luxurious passenger cars for railways. By 1893, more than 12,000 people lived in the town called Pullman, worked in George's factories, bought goods at his company stores, and paid rent to his company.

A westward view from atop Market Hall in the town of Pullman. In the right background is the Arcade building, which was one of the United States' first indoor shopping centers.

ROBOT JUNCTION

Boilerplate first intersected with Pullman at the World's Columbian Exposition, where a specially built train of Pullman train cars and a scaled-down replica of George's town were displayed in the Transportation Building. The mechanical man visited the Pullman exhibits and staged a show of strength by pulling one of the cars 1,000 yards.

"The feature of the Pullman exhibit that draws crowds is the train, with its rich furnishings, wonderful and plentiful carving, and conveniences that characterize palaces instead of public coaches ordinarily. The locomotive is a duplicate of the one which has attained a speed of ninety-seven miles an hour, and its coaches are said to weigh 90,000 pounds each. Great amazement has been expressed by visitors who witnessed Professor Campion's automaton act in the locomotive's stead, drawing a coach behind it for the better part of a mile without assistance."

—Henry Davenport Northrop, *Pictorial History of the World's Fair*

DOWNSIZING

Pullman was touted as a model town, drawing thousands of adventurous sightseers during the world's fair. Even Lily Campion paid a visit and lunched at the Hotel Florence. Beneath the surface, though, Pullman was no utopia.

On top of the profits from his company, George demanded a 6 percent profit from his town, so rents and utility charges were higher in Pullman than in nearby neighborhoods. Workers were not allowed to own homes in Pullman; they had no choice but to rent, and they could be evicted or laid off at any time. Pullman agents could enter, inspect, and alter their homes—at the workers' expense, without their permission. Pullman spotters reported any resident who violated company policies.

"About the only difference between slavery at Pullman and what it was down South before the war, is that there the owners took care of the slaves when they were sick and here they don't."

—Anonymous Pullman worker, quoted in the *Chicago Herald* (May 31, 1890)

The chain of events that drew Boilerplate more deeply into the Pullman story began with the financial Panic of 1893 and the depression that ensued. When George's business fell off, he laid off workers and cut wages—without reducing rents or water charges. Rent was deducted from paychecks, leaving many Pullman employees without enough money to buy food. Some were forced into perpetual debt to the company. Company stockholders still received their guaranteed 8 percent profit, though.

⬆ Boilerplate pulls one of Pullman's famous sleeper cars, the ultimate in luxury and high-tech rail transportation of the day, at the Chicago World's Columbian Exposition in 1893.

⬆⬆ Archie Campion's sister, Lily, stayed at the world-class Hotel Florence, named after George Pullman's daughter, during a tour of Pullman town. Lily supported the railroad tycoon's stated intent to raise the quality of life among laborers, but she recognized that Pullman's company town was far from a utopian dream—it was, in fact, an economic prison for many workers.

⬆ A residential street in Pullman. Its seemingly idyllic appearance does not betray the oppressive aspects of a company town. Today, Pullman is a neighborhood on the south side of Chicago.

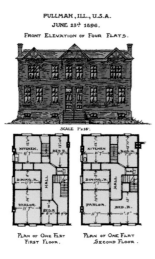

PULLMAN, ILL., U.S.A.
JUNE 23ᴿᴰ 1896.
FRONT ELEVATION OF FOUR FLATS.

SCALE 1"=16'.

PLAN OF ONE FLAT
FIRST FLOOR.

PLAN OF ONE FLAT
SECOND FLOOR.

Plans for a typical two-story four-flat that housed workers in Pullman town. The living room was 11 x 14', with 7 x 13' and 6 x 10' bedrooms.

The National Guard was among the armed forces sent to Chicago to protect railroads during the Pullman strike.

STRIKE!

By May 1894, Pullman workers had reached the breaking point. George refused to negotiate or offer any relief, so they voted to strike. In June they won support from the American Railway Union (ARU), a national organization headed by former railroad fireman Eugene Debs. Within weeks, the nation's railroads were all but paralyzed. The cost of groceries and other goods soared in Chicago.

What began as a peaceful, organized strike for better wages turned nasty after President Grover Cleveland ordered the U.S. Army into Chicago on July 3, despite Illinois Governor John Altgeld's strong objections. It was an unprecedented move.

Archie paid scant attention to these events until July 5, when an unexplained fire burned down seven buildings on the Columbian Exposition grounds—including Machinery Hall, the site of Boilerplate's public debut. Although the fire's cause was never conclusively proven, inflammatory newspaper accounts blamed striking Pullman workers.

An editorial cartoon unfavorably depicting labor leader Eugene Debs as a tyrant, during the Pullman Strike of 1894.

BLOOD ON THE TRACKS

By this time, Chicago was littered with armed encampments of 6,000 federal and state troops, 3,100 police, and 5,000 deputy marshals. The deputies were a motley assortment of hastily recruited civilians, unpredictable at best and brutal at worst, paid by the railroads. Large crowds of unemployed, angry men had joined the strikers. The conflict spun out of control, goaded by sensationalistic press.

At Governor Altgeld's request, Archie agreed to let Boilerplate be attached to Company H of the 2nd Regiment of the Illinois National Guard, in hopes that the metal man could help curb the escalating violence. On July 7, 1894, Boilerplate and Company H attempted to disperse a crowd that was blocking a train at 49th and Loomis. When the crowd grew unruly, the junior officer in command first ordered a bayonet charge, then told his men to fire at will. In the end, it was the strike's bloodiest incident: At least four civilians were killed, and twenty wounded.

Company H of the Illinois National Guard's 2nd Regiment encamped in Pullman town during the Pullman strike. In the background are Boilerplate, Archie Campion, and Edward Fullerton, as well as a distinctive Pullman factory building. July 6, 1894.

"NEVER AGAIN"

Boilerplate didn't inflict any casualties, and in fact there's evidence that the robot protected a woman and child who were in the line of fire. Nevertheless, Archie, chagrined by his creation's participation in this awful event, immediately removed Boilerplate from military control.

"I am mortified by the knowledge that my mechanical soldier was pitted against honest workingmen and blameless bystanders. Government has every right to secure public safety—but not by slaughtering the public itself. Never again will a creation of mine be used in an action against the American populace."

—Archibald Campion, letter to Nikola Tesla (July 8, 1894)

Months later, after Debs had been arrested, the strike broken, and George scolded by the federal Strike Commission, Jane Addams and Lily took Archie to visit the town of Pullman. Its residents eventually overcame their distrust of the wealthy Campions and showed them what life was really like there. Archie and Lily became lifelong benefactors, even after the town was subsumed into Chicago.

"It is a treason against the human soul to profit from the suffering and privation of those less fortunate. Prosperity for the few need not come at the cost of misery for the masses."

—Lily Campion, "The Sin of Heedless Prosperity," *The Chicago Chronicle* (May 14, 1894)

The strike survivors never quite trusted Boilerplate, though. In their eyes, the robot was a walking embodiment of the combined political, financial, and military might that had been wielded against them.

Of all Boilerplate's adventures, this was the only one that Archie regretted for the rest of his life.

Archie gave permission for Boilerplate to be attached to the National Guard. That decision weighed heavily on his conscience after guardsmen fired on a crowd blocking a train at 49th and Loomis.

In this engraving from *Harper's Weekly*, Boilerplate rescues a young woman as the Illinois National Guard opens fire on a crowd of Pullman strikers and other demonstrators.

EUGENE DEBS

1855–1926

"Years ago I recognized my kinship with all living things, and I made up my mind that I was not one bit better than the meanest on the earth. I said then and I say now, that while there is a lower class, I am in it; while there is a criminal element, I am of it; while there is a soul in prison, I am not free."
    —Eugene V. Debs

Eugene Debs—a founder of the modern labor union and five-time presidential candidate—was born in the American heartland in Terre Haute, Indiana, the son of immigrants. At fourteen, he left school and started working on the railroads.

Later he helped organize unions such as the American Railway Union and the Industrial Workers of the World. Debs saw Boilerplate as a potential threat to human workers' livelihood, and he urged Archie to limit the robot to only the most dangerous of occupations.

After the Pullman strike, Debs was jailed for six months. Upon his release, 100,000 cheering supporters greeted him in person. Formerly a moderate, he became radicalized by what he perceived as President Cleveland's abuse of power. Of his five presidential bids, Debs made especially strong showings in the 1912 and 1920 elections. His 1920 campaign was run from prison because he had been jailed again, for protesting U.S. involvement in World War I in 1918.

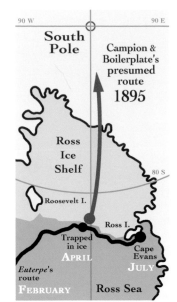

Boilerplate and Archie on the deck of the *Euterpe* as it navigates the Ross Sea during their Antarctic expedition. The kennels built into the sides of the ship housed sled dogs.

expedition, the *Challenger* journey of 1872–76. Perhaps daunted by the icy continent's newly recognized vastness, explorers avoided it for almost two decades after that.

SEA OF ICE

Archie and Boilerplate set sail in February 1895 on the *Euterpe,* an iron-hulled merchant vessel. The ship approached Antarctica from the Ross Sea. As it neared the Ross Ice Shelf, it was surrounded and eventually trapped by pack ice. The crew resigned themselves to spending a long, dark, frigid winter there, awaiting the spring thaw.

VOYAGE TO THE BOTTOM OF THE WORLD

In 1895, almost two years after introducing Boilerplate to the public, Professor Archibald Campion embarked on the first field trial to test his creation's abilities in an extreme environment: He took Boilerplate to Antarctica.

MYSTERIOUS ISLAND

The earliest recorded sightings of Antarctica date back to 1820. At first it was thought to be an island or archipelago. Seafaring nations tentatively explored its edges, hoping to find a way around it to the South Pole—and perhaps new trade routes as well.

Sir James Ross determined in 1840 that the pole lay inland somewhere, inaccessible by ship. His suspicions that Antarctica was a continent were confirmed by the first scientific oceanic

Boilerplate pulls Archie's sled toward the South Pole.

With time on his hands, Archie decided to make a solo attempt to reach the South Pole, using Boilerplate as his sled-puller. Over the adamant protestations of the *Euterpe*'s

Boilerplate at the bottom of the world, April 1895.

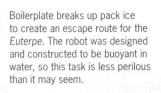

Boilerplate breaks up pack ice to create an escape route for the *Euterpe*. The robot was designed and constructed to be buoyant in water, so this task is less perilous than it may seem.

Captain Edmund Bentine, the professor and his robot departed and soon vanished over the horizon.

"I am certain that the beleaguered Bentine believed me lost, a frozen corpse laid out beside an inoperative machine. But I knew I could succeed with the aid of my metal man, and I could not bear to forgo the opportunity to visit the very end of the Earth."

—Archibald Campion, letter to Edward Fullerton (October 15, 1895)

Boilerplate and its inventor reappeared at the *Euterpe* two weeks later. Archie was in decent physical condition, but surprisingly quiet about whether he had reached the pole. In later years, he excused himself by saying that without any physical evidence of his accomplishment, he couldn't claim to have performed such a feat.

"THE UTMOST DISPATCH"

After five months, the pack ice thawed and shifted enough for Boilerplate to carve out a channel that the *Euterpe* could escape through. The expedition arrived at Cape Evans in summer 1895.

"The intermittent snow-squalls grew less frequent. In a lull of the storm the professor's iron man completed its task, upon which we set sail with the utmost dispatch. We got clear of the channel just in the nick of time to see two ice floes come together with a splitting, pulverizing crash behind us; but we were safe and in a very few minutes were at last in open water again."

—From the diary of William Wolfe, first mate of the *Euterpe* (June 1895)

News of Archie's expedition inspired a wave of public fascination with Antarctica but, ironically, did little to stimulate interest in Boilerplate. England, not to be bested by the upstart American and his metal marionette, convened the 1895 International Geographical Congress and revived British resolve to plant a Union Jack on the South Pole. The planet was starting to run out of unexplored territory, after all.

In 1899, Carsten Borchgrevink sailed from Australia to Antarctica aboard the *Southern Cross*, survived an Antarctic winter, yet failed to reach the pole. English expeditions met similar fates and worse. On January 9, 1909, Ernest Shackleton passed within 160 kilometers of the South Pole. In 1912, Robert Scott died during his polar trek. A Norwegian, Roald Amundsen, went down in history as the first man to reach the South Pole on December 14, 1911.

They all followed the route pioneered by Archie Campion.

THE LAST QUEEN OF HAWAII 1838–1917

After his Antarctic adventure, Archie defrosted in Hawaii, where Lily was vacationing. Boilerplate was a huge hit with the native Polynesians, who developed a comical hula dance based on the robot's strange sounds and movements.

Archie soon learned that Lily had (as she was wont to do) taken up the cause of a political underdog: Lili'uokalani, the last Queen of Hawaii, convicted of conspiring to overthrow Hawaii's provisional government.

BUSINESS AS USUAL

The *provisional government* was a group of American businessmen who had overthrown the Hawaiian monarchy. They and other wealthy immigrants wanted to secure their land ownership and control the sugar cane trade. So, in 1887, they forced Lili'uokalani's brother and predecessor, King David Kalakaua, to enact the Bayonet Constitution, which stripped power from the native Hawaiian rulers and took away voting rights from most of the native people.

The Queen of Hawaii was ousted in a U.S.-backed coup by Sanford Dole and a small group of businessmen.

Lili'uokalani inherited the throne in 1891. She rejected the Bayonet Constitution and tried to restore power to the Hawaiian crown and people. In 1893 the so-called Citizens' Committee of Public Safety, led by lawyer and newspaper publisher Lorrin Thurston, deposed her and seized control of the formerly sovereign nation.

The Americans declared themselves in charge and renamed the country the *Republic of Hawaii*. Thurston appointed Sanford Dole, whose family would later become world-famous pineapple moguls, president of the new republic.

THE CAPTIVE QUEEN

In 1895, Lili'uokalani was arrested on charges of plotting a revolt, put on trial, and sentenced to five years' imprisonment. With Archie's help, Lily got the queen paroled less than a year later, then finally pardoned in 1896.

In 1898, during the Spanish-American War, the United States annexed Hawaii. Dole continued to rule it as governor until 1903. The native Hawaiian monarchy never regained control of its own land.

Left to right: Boilerplate, Lily Campion, Archie Campion, the Queen, and a U.S. Marine.
"On the 6th of September [1895], about eight months after my arrest, I was notified by Colonel McLean that he was no longer responsible for my custody, and that at three o'clock that afternoon I might leave the palace. So a carriage was called, and I was driven from the doors of the beautiful edifice which they now style the Executive Building. In company with my advocates, the Campions, and their peculiar metal servant, I was driven to the gateway at Washington Place, my earlier home.
"My pardon, as it was called, arrived at a later date. All the intervening time I was supposed to be under parole, and could have been arrested and recommitted at any moment."
—Lili'uokalani, Queen of Hawaii, *Hawaii's Story by Hawaii's Queen* (1898)

ELECTION '96

Archie Campion and Boilerplate ham it up in a lively political parade for Democratic nominee William Jennings Bryan during the 1896 presidential campaign. Archie considered himself a patriot who supported smart policies, not a loyalist who blindly backed political parties. Thus he could support both a Democrat such as Bryan and a Republican such as Teddy Roosevelt—a stance that might seem contradictory in today's climate of partisan conflict.

Although Bryan's populist beliefs strongly appealed to Archie, the agnostic scientist disagreed with the politician's religious views. Three decades later, in 1925, Archie lost all respect for his former political ally when a high school teacher named John Scopes was put on trial for teaching evolution in a Tennessee high school. Bryan, an avid opponent of Darwinism, was the lead prosecutor. He faced legendary defense attorney Clarence Darrow in what became known as the *Scopes Monkey Trial*.

THE FIRST AUTO RACE

Boilerplate and spectators in front of the Palace of Fine Arts in Jackson Park, where the race began.

Frank Duryea and his winning race car.

Archie Campion participated in the first American automobile race on Thanksgiving Day, November 28, 1895, in Chicago. He lost to Frank Duryea, who drove a vehicle designed by Frank and his brother Charles. Duryea won the fifty-five-mile race in seven hours and fifty-three minutes.

The course began on the city's south side, running up to the adjoining town of Evanston on the north, then back. Out of eleven entrants, six vehicles actually started the race, and only two finished: Archie's and Frank's.

The *Chicago Times-Herald* sponsored the event, putting up $5,000 in prize money and promoting it for almost a year in advance. In the newspaper's contest to name the new horseless carriage, the term *motorcycle* won—but competing papers refused to use the word, and it never caught on.

The first internal combustion-powered American automobile was designed by George Selden in 1877, but German engineers took the lead in the 1880s. By the time of the famous Chicago race, most of the entries were German-made cars. The only two American autos were those built by the Duryea brothers and Archie Campion.

Boilerplate won this contest of speed with the Duryea brothers, who won America's first automobile race in 1895.

COLONIAL AFRICA

EMPIRE OF ETHIOPIA

FRANCE
BRITAIN
ITALY
GERMANY
BELGIUM
PORTUGAL
SPAIN

AFRICAN ADVENTURES

Boilerplate and Archie spent much of 1896–97 in northern Africa. They went there at the invitation of Italy's Premier Francesco Crispi, who had seen Boilerplate at the World's Columbian Exposition. Crispi requested a field demonstration of the mechanical soldier in Ethiopia.

THE SCRAMBLE FOR AFRICA

For decades, European governments had been tussling over who would control which region in Africa. Italy grabbed two coastal countries on the Horn of Africa: Eritrea and Somalia. They were inconveniently separated by the ancient kingdom of Ethiopia—one of only two remaining independent African nations—so Italy tried to grab Ethiopia, too.

"Tesla holds a poor opinion of the Italians and advises against any dealings with them. I must ignore his advice this once. What luck that I shall have occasion to concurrently test my mechanical man in a desert environment and demonstrate its potential to preserve human life by substituting for men in military conflicts."

—Archibald Campion, letter to Mark Twain (February 21, 1896)

But Boilerplate's opportunity for desert combat didn't materialize on this trip. By the time Archie and the robot reached their rendezvous point in Cairo, the Italian invaders were getting trounced by Ethiopian troops at the Battle of Adwa. Crispi resigned from office within days.

UNEARTHING HISTORY

His plans derailed, Archie opted to explore. Egypt was under British control, and Cairo

The Campions soak up some ancient history. The professor and his robot assisted the Egyptian Geological Survey with archaeological excavations in 1896.

A Sudanese colonial cavalryman with his steed and Campion's Marvel. Since the days of the sixteenth-century Spanish conquistador Hernán Cortés, European powers had found various ways of using native peoples to help seize new colonies. Often the locals were conscripted into the invading nation's army. Another tactic was to exploit local conflicts, pitting one native faction against another until they so weakened each other that the colonizers could easily take control.

about his new assignment as Director of Sudan Railways, Percy talked Archie into letting Boilerplate help him build railroads across the desert. The metal man's mission was to lay at least a mile of track every day.

Girouard was part of the Anglo-Egyptian Nile Expeditionary Force: 17,200 Egyptian and 8,600 British soldiers commanded by Gen. Horatio Herbert Kitchener, *sirdar* of the Egyptian army. Kitchener had just launched a campaign against native Islamic forces in Sudan. A decade earlier, the Sudanese had driven the British out of Sudan and killed Gen. Charles Gordon, a popular hero and a comrade of Kitchener's.

had been practically flooded with Europeans ever since the Suez Canal opened in 1869. Archie and Boilerplate connected with the fledgling Egyptian Geological Survey, working on digs with English archaeologists W.M. Flinders Petrie and James Quibell.

"The Pharaonic town stood on the borders of the desert about 300 yards from the canal. Mr. Quibell cleared out the ruins of the temple in which the Horus of the locality was worshipped. From among millions of potsherds he has extracted wonderful things—a gold falcon's head, two copper statues of the Pharaoh Pioupi I, a delicate statuette in lapis-lazuli. One of his aides in recovering these antiquities is, by contrast, the embodiment of modernity: the anthropomorphic machine constructed by Prof. Campion."

—C.K. Hollingworth, "Egypt: Ancient Sites and Modern Scenes," *International Review,* Vol. 3, No. 6 (1896)

DESERT TRACKS

At around the same time, an old acquaintance of Archie's showed up in Egypt: Percy Girouard, a Canadian railway engineer serving in the British army. Flush with excitement

"ARROGANCE ITSELF"

Initially, Kitchener's goal was to retake the northern Sudanese city of Dongola, in a show of force to demonstrate support for the faltering Italians. But Kitchener didn't stop after capturing Dongola in September 1896; instead, he kept going deeper into Sudan.

Archie, absorbed in the engineering challenges of Girouard's railroad project and in keeping sand from fouling up Boilerplate's works, was temporarily oblivious to the larger political and military context.

"You will call me naïve again, and you are right to do so. I allowed Percy to sway me with notions of grand adventure and achievement—and it is true that we achieved the grand adventure of surviving sandstorm, flood, and cholera. As for the railway, I fear all we have achieved is to advance British territorial ambition and Kitchener's personal quest for vengeance. This war is arrogance itself."

—Archibald Campion, letter to Lily Campion (December 1896)

SOUDAN

TS & WARLIKE EPISODES.

General Horatio Herbert Kitchener, 1897.

KITCHENER OF KHARTOUM

Boilerplate and Archie parted ways with Kitchener before he reconquered Khartoum, the site of Gordon's slaying. Many years and several wars later, they would encounter him again as Great Britain's Secretary of State for War in the early days of World War I. By then, Lord Kitchener of Khartoum, or *K. of K.*, was one of the most famous military leaders in British history.

Kitchener's success in Sudan rested heavily on the railroads Boilerplate helped build. Future British Prime Minister Winston Churchill, who served in the Sudan campaign, wrote: *"Fighting the Dervishes was primarily a matter of transport. Khalifa was conquered on the railway. For that we owe thanks to a French-Canadian lieutenant and an American automaton."*

This colorful rendering of British Gen. Horatio Herbert Kitchener's 1896–98 Sudan campaign is a poster advertising a theatrical re-creation. Stage versions of real events were a common form of entertainment in the days before moving pictures, though of course they lacked the dramatic explosions and expansive scenery shown here.

Boilerplate never participated in infantry charges such as the one in this poster. Rather, the robot helped build the rail line depicted at the top of the illustration, in the background. The railroad was laid by the Anglo-Egyptian army to transport men and supplies through the inhospitable desert. Boilerplate's contribution was praised by Winston Churchill, who served under Kitchener in the Sudan.

GOLD! GOLD! GOLD!

In June 1897, a company called Oregon Boiler Works contacted Archie Campion to propose that his mechanical man make a publicity appearance in the Canadian mining boom town of Dawson City, all expenses paid. Curious to see the northern frontier after exploring Antarctica and Africa, Archie set out for the Yukon with Boilerplate.

The Scales was a tent village where goods were weighed before stampeders continued on to Dawson City. Boilerplate is partially loaded for an ascent up the Golden Stairs—the rough-hewn, icy mountain trail in the background, dotted with a seemingly endless line of climbers.

NEWLY MINTED MILLIONAIRES

Not long after Archie departed, a bunch of scruffy but happy miners returned from Canada, toting bags and barrels stuffed full of gold. They had struck it rich in the Klondike River valley—exactly where the professor and his robot were headed.

An epidemic of gold fever spread like the flu. Headlines around the world screamed *"GOLD! GOLD! GOLD!"* and thousands flocked to West Coast cities to book passage north. Thus began the legendary Klondike Gold Rush.

9195—Preparing to Climb "The Golden Stair" and Peterson's Trail, Chilkoot Pass, Alaska.

STAMPEDER'S SUPPLY LIST

Klondikers brought along a ton of goods because they had to. The Canadian government wouldn't let anyone across the border into the Yukon Territory without a year's worth of supplies per person.

There were almost as many sources of supply lists as there were stampeders. Every store was ready with a checklist and inflated prices. Slapdash instruction manuals also proliferated, many written by city slickers who had never set foot in the Yukon.

The following list is attributed to the report of the Governor of Alaska for 1897.

OUTFIT FOR TWO MEN FOR 14 MONTHS, ALASKA PRICES

⊷ ⧓ ⊷

4 barrels best flour, at $6	$24.00
200 pounds granulated sugar, at 6 cents	12.00
200 pounds navy beans, at 4 cents	8.00
100 pounds of corn meal	2.75
250 pounds of breakfast bacon, at 12.5 cents	31.25
75 pounds of island rice, 6 cents	4.50
2 cases condensed milk	17.50
20 pounds of salt	0.35
25 pounds best Mocha and Java coffee	8.75
10 pounds best tea	4.50
8 pounds soda	0.70
20 pounds baking powder	9.20
25 pounds dried apricots	2.50
25 pounds dried peaches	2.50
25 pounds dried apples	2.25
2 boxes candles	5.00
1 box pepper, 25 cents;	
soap $1	1.25
3 boxes yeast, 25 cents;	
one-half tin of matches, 50 cents	0.75
1 Yukon stove complete	6.00
3 half-spring shovels	3.00
3 miner's picks	3.00
1 double-bladed ax complete	1.50
13 oil sacks, 50's and 100's	7.55
2 gold pans, $1; one coffee mill, 35 cents	1.35
12 condensed onions	5.00
10 pounds evaporated spuds	2.50
40 pounds rope	5.00
Toilet soap	0.50
6 tin plates, 50 cents; 3 granite cups, 50 cents	1.00
1 coffee pot, 40 cents; whetstone, 20 cents	0.60
Awls, shoe thread, wax, bristles, etc.	1.00
2 fry pans, $1.00; fish line and hooks, 50 cents	1.50
2 - extract of beef	1.00
6 assorted files, 60 cents; oil blacking, 50 cents	1.10
1 package chocolate	0.30
2 miner's candlesticks	1.00
1 iron brace and bits	1.75
24 pounds of raisins	2.40

OUTFIT FOR BOAT

⊷ ⧓ ⊷

30 pounds nails, $1.50;	
5 pounds white lead, 60 cents	2.10
Candle wicking, 20 cents; 1 2-inch auger, $1.25	1.45
Oakum, 25 cents; pitch, 25 cents	0.50
1 hand saw, $1.50; 1 jack pane, 75 cents	2.25
Paint brush, 25 cents; 4 candle wicks, 40 cents	0.65
2 pairs oars, $1.75; oarlocks, 40 cents	2.15
3 pairs heavy wool blankets	20.50
2 pairs pack straps, $3.00; 1 hand ax, $1.00	4.00
2 pairs hip rubber boots, leather soles, $6.00	12.00
2 pairs high top lace shoes	3.00
4 pairs German socks 75 cents	3.00
2 pairs lumberman's rubbers	3.00
2 pairs suspenders	0.75
4 suits heavy wool underwear	12.00
4 dark blue flannel overshirts	8.00
4 pairs Mackinaw pants	11.00
2 Mackinaw coats	6.00
2 blanket coats	8.00
12 pairs wool socks	4.50
6 pairs wool mittens	3.00
40 yards mosquito netting	1.00
11 buckskin pouches	5.00
1 magnet, 50 cents; 2 pairs goggles, 50 cents	1.00
2 pairs snow glasses	1.00
1 dozen bandana handkerchiefs	1.00
1 lot spoons, knives and forks	1.35
1 butcher knife	0.75
4 oil blankets	6.00
1 lot buckets, pans, cooking utensils, etc.	3.35
2 sou'westers, $1.00; tent, $12.00	13.00
1 41 Colt revolver and ammunition	15.00
1 Winchester rifle and ammunition	18.00
2 fur caps	2.50
1 whipsaw	5.50

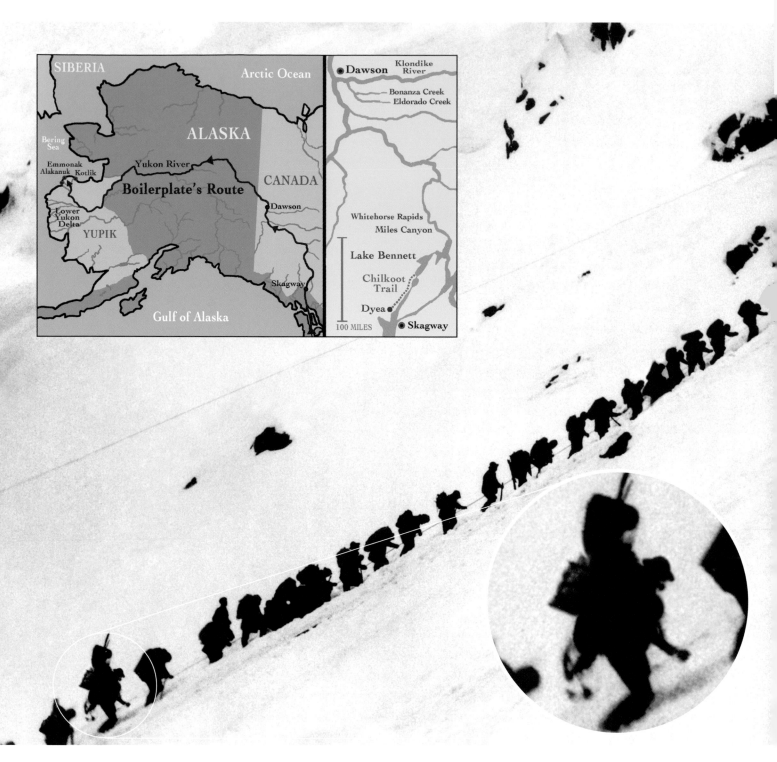

Each stampeder made as many as forty back-breaking trips up and down the Golden Stairs, just to get their supplies to the pass at the summit. Boilerplate did it in only a dozen trips.

"HEART-BREAKING LABORS"

Archie and Boilerplate arrived in Dyea, Alaska, with the first wave of *stampeders* or *Klondikers*, as they were called. They faced a long, arduous trek across formidable mountains to Dawson City. During the next year, more than 100,000 stampeders would try, but only about a third of them would make it to Dawson.

The first obstacle was just getting their gear up the mountain. Well-prepared prospectors brought along an entire year's worth of supplies, or roughly 2,000 pounds of goods per person. They had to haul their outfit up the steep trails bit by bit, in dozens of back-and-forth trips. The trails were littered with abandoned possessions, cast off in desperation.

"Of all heart-breaking labors, that of breaking trail is the worst. At every step the great webbed shoe sinks till the snow is level with the knee. Then up, straight up, the deviation of a fraction of an inch being a certain precursor of disaster, the snowshoe must be lifted till the surface is cleared; then forward, down, and the other foot is raised perpendicularly for the matter of half a yard. He who tries this for the first time, if happily he measures not his length on the treacherous footing, will give up exhausted at the end of a hundred yards. He who travels the Long Trail with an unflagging machine-servant such as Campion's is a man whom the gods may envy."

—Jack London, "The White Silence," *Overland Monthly,* Vol. 33 (February 1899)

UP THE GOLDEN STAIRCASE

The professor made swift progress thanks to Boilerplate's strength, endurance, and Antarctic experience. They ascended via the 33-mile Chilkoot Trail, which crested in an almost vertical climb up 1,500 steps hacked out of the icy snow, known as the *Golden Staircase.* On the other side of Chilkoot Pass, the trails led down to Lake Bennett, which drains into the Yukon River.

Boilerplate with a group of Canadian Mounties. The gold-rush town of Dawson City was in Canada, but the exact location of the U.S.–Canada border in this area was under dispute. Canada's North West Mounted Police nevertheless set up customs stations at Chilkoot Pass, backed up by the 200-man Yukon Field Force, which assisted in guarding prisoners and gold shipments. The boundary dispute was finally resolved by international arbitration in 1903.

"NO SNAKES IN THE KLONDYKE? THAT SHOWS 'TWAS GOD'S PLAN TO GIVE TO THE SNAKE BETTER SENSE THAN TO MAN."

—Anonymous

Luckily, Archie and his automaton arrived before winter set in. They built a boat at Lake Bennett, then navigated the Yukon River down to Dawson without incident. Klondikers who got there after the waterways froze had a long wait in store. That winter, a tent city of 10,000 people huddled at the summit, waiting for the Yukon to thaw.

LAND OF THE YUP'IK

Boilerplate poses with two Yup'ik
women from the village of Kotlik.

Archie's main interest in the Klondike was exploring, not
prospecting for gold. He and Boilerplate followed the Yukon
River to its delta at the Bering Sea. There they befriended
the native Yup'ik Eskimo and stayed in the villages of Kotlik,
Emmonak, and Alakanuk. The tribes welcomed him with

generous hospitality and regarded Boilerplate as a
white man's oddity—interesting, but of little practical use.
Although Archie crisscrossed the globe and visited many
exotic locales, his travels in the Yukon ranked among his
favorite experiences.

THE BOILER MAN

Up until this time, Archie's creation was usually dubbed *Professor Campion's Mechanical Marvel,* or some such ornate epithet, in written accounts. It was the Dawson City newspaper that christened the robot *Boilerplate* after it appeared in Oregon Boiler Works advertisements.

"Dawson City is something I thought I should never see: It is the raw frontier, a town taking shape, a jumble of constantly shifting tents, cabins, and mud. Fortunes rise and fall by the hour; millionaires and paupers stand in the same queue awaiting their mail. And everywhere throngs of men mill about, lacking any sense of what to do now they've arrived. It strikes me as an especially sorry sight in comparison to the communal cooperation that prevails in the native Eskimo villages I visited.

"Certain goods are in such short supply that rather than burn a candle, I write to you by the light of my automaton's electrical eyes. Despite this dearth, already there have been erected in Dawson dance halls, gambling parlors, and saloons to part the careless miner from his hard-won gold. There is even a newspaper of sorts, the Klondike Nugget, *that has assigned to my mechanical man the questionable sobriquet of 'Boilerplate' and to myself, 'The Boiler Man.'"*

—Archibald Campion, letter to Lily Campion (February 1898)

Archie Campion and Boilerplate pose with a draft horse team that was used to transport giant steam boilers, the primary power source in the Klondike.

FOOL'S GOLD

With the spring melt in 1898, thousands more fortune-seekers stampeded into Dawson City. It quickly ballooned from a small fishing outpost into a city of 40,000. Food became so scarce and expensive that scurvy, malnutrition, and famine were constant threats.

Alas, for most stampeders there was another harsh irony waiting at the end of the trail. The first big strike had occurred a year earlier, so all the land worth mining had been claimed before the rush even started. Newcomers, including a then unknown Jack London, wearily staggered into the Klondike only to learn that there was no reason for them to stay. London was at least lucky enough to be a talented writer whose tales of rugged Yukon life later launched his career.

"Men, on arrival here, have suddenly found out the unlimited opportunities for getting rich will not be reached no matter how great their capacity for enduring work and hardships."

—Stampeder Alfred McMichael, letter to Hattie McMichael (August 1898)

By the time the stampede peaked, Archie was already steaming southward with Boilerplate. He started packing as soon as he heard the big news—the United States was at war with Spain!

"If you insist on getting your fool self and your walking tin can blown to smithereens in battle, then here is your chance. Word has it that the irrepressible Mr. Roosevelt is bound for Cuba, sword in hand."

—Mark Twain, letter to Archie Campion (March 17, 1898)

Boilerplate stands outside the Portland Market at the north end of Dawson City's main thoroughfare, spring 1898. Dawson was the last great gold-rush town. The era of the rugged individual frontier prospector was nearly at an end; soon, large mining companies would move in.

THE PHOTOGRAPHER

Robert Stewart was a successful photographer and friend to the Campions. He often accompanied and documented Boilerplate on its travels, including visits to Asia, Alaska, and Antarctica. His specialty was 3-D stereo photography, which was wildly popular at the turn of the century. Stereo prints were viewed with handheld wood-and-tin stereopticons. All the stereo images that Boilerplate appears in—and in fact most surviving photographs of the robot—were taken by Stewart.

Souvenir postcards of Boilerplate with Robert Stewart in 1903, attending the fortieth anniversary commemoration of the Battle of Gettysburg. For the occasion, Stewart is dressed in the uniform worn by his father, Harold, who fought at Gettysburg in the Union cavalry under Gen. John Buford.

A MAN, A PLAN, A CANAL

The canal was a crowning glory for the President, hailed as the greatest boon to international trade in modern times.

When Teddy Roosevelt decided to personally inspect the Panama Canal construction zone in November 1906, he invited Archie Campion to accompany him and evaluate the methods, designs, and equipment being used. Archie hoped to also demonstrate Boilerplate's potential usefulness as a construction worker under conditions too dangerous for humans.

"With intense energy men and machines do their task, the white men supervising matters and handling the machines, while the tens of thousands of black men do the rough manual labor where it is not worth while to have machines do it. It is an epic feat, and one of immense significance."

—Theodore Roosevelt, letter to Kermit Roosevelt (November 20, 1906)

FROM SEA TO SHINING SEA

Before the Panama Canal was dug, the only way to get from the Atlantic Ocean to the Pacific Ocean (or vice versa) by sea was to travel thousands of extra miles around South America. Pretty much everyone wanted to find a faster route.

The canal zone was originally part of Colombia. Construction of the canal was started in 1880 by a French company, which went bankrupt and stopped work in 1889. In 1903, egged on by French and American business interests, and backed up by U.S. military forces, Panama declared its independence from Colombia. The U.S. State Department promptly recognized Panama as a new nation, and work on the canal resumed under U.S. control the next year.

The Panama Canal opened to traffic in 1914, suddenly bringing New York 8,000 miles closer to San Francisco. At the end of 1999, control of the canal was handed over to the Panamanian government. It's still a crucial trade route today.

CONSTRUCTION COSTS

The various construction companies involved over the years employed a total of about 80,000 workers. Approximately 27,500 of them died,

Teddy Roosevelt, wearing a tropical white suit, surveys progress on the Panama Canal with Boilerplate. T. R.'s trip to Panama was the first time a sitting U.S. President visited a foreign country.

many from malaria and yellow fever. Archie was appalled by the mounting death toll, but he failed to convince contractors that a robot could serve their needs.

"Again the cost of manufacturing mechanical workers is cited as prohibitive. How many men here have fallen victim to disease or mud-slide? Why is this human loss not deemed 'prohibitive'? I despair of finding an industry that places as great a value on a man's life as it does on monetary profit. Perhaps, as Twain holds, this is in the very nature of the corporation—it is an abstraction, not a person. It lacks mind, soul, and heart.

"Boilerplate will not find favor with the captains of industry, so long as there be an inexhaustible supply of humanity rendered desperate by circumstance. Which is to say, never. And so I must change tack. No longer shall I seek to license my invention as a laborer. Until the day when good sense prevails upon our captains of state to put my mechanical man to its proper military use, it shall serve the greater good by taking such action as may bring relief to the suffering or aid in drawing the public eye to injustice."

—Archibald Campion, letter to Frank Reade Jr. (November 20, 1906)

"[W]hat we do now will be of consequence, not merely decades, but centuries hence, and we must be sure that we are taking the right step before we act."

—President Theodore Roosevelt, letter to Secretary of State John Hay (August 19, 1903)

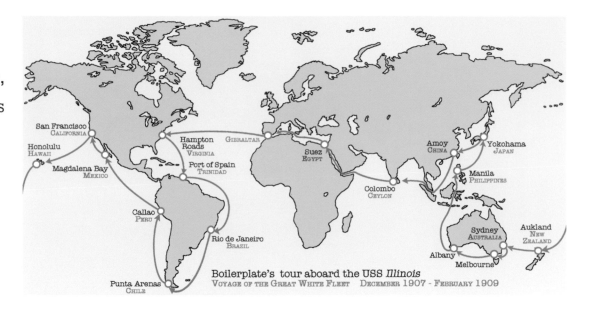

Boilerplate's tour aboard the USS *Illinois*
VOYAGE OF THE GREAT WHITE FLEET   DECEMBER 1907 – FEBRUARY 1909

AROUND THE WORLD BY BATTLESHIP

From December 1907 through February 1909, Archie Campion and Boilerplate went on a 43,000-mile cruise with the U.S. Navy. Along with 14,000 sailors and marines, they circum- navigated the planet in the historic voyage of the Atlantic Fleet, later dubbed the *Great White Fleet*. They made twenty stops on six conti- nents—and the world turned out to greet them.

ROBOT COP

In 1907, Archie's friend Robert Stewart convinced him to try out Boilerplate as a policeman. The robot was assigned to a beat patrol in the Levee District, Chicago's center of vice. Patronized by all classes and colors, the neighborhood was home to an as- sortment of drug dens and brothels, including the world-famous Everleigh Club. This ultra-opulent brothel, run by the Everleigh sisters, served statesmen and celebrities from the Prince of Prussia to Jack Johnson.

Bribery kept the very lucra- tive, and very illegal, activities in the Levee going. Boilerplate was an incorruptible cop, however, and eventually began to seriously disrupt busi- ness. The Levee was part of Chicago's First Ward, run by Alderman Michael "Hinky Dink" Kenna. He had Boilerplate removed from the police force after only six months. His ward colleague Alderman "Bathhouse John" Coughlin was highly entertained by Boilerplate, but not enough to suffer cuts in his kickbacks.

A fanciful 1907 cartoon of Boilerplate engaged in a police raid in the Levee District.

Aldermen Kenna and Coughlin ruled Chicago's Levee District from the 1890s to the 1930s. At their bac- chanalian annual fundraiser, the First Ward Ball, raunchy sexual displays and transvestism were routine. It often ended in a drunken riot. Attendees included politicians, busi- nessmen, gamblers, and prostitutes. The party ran yearly from 1897 to 1909, by which time it had grown to 15,000 revelers and was shut down by the mayor. Hinky Dink called it a *lallapalooza*.

President Teddy Roosevelt and Boilerplate offer salutations to the Great White Fleet from aboard the USS *Illinois*, just before the fleet departs on its unprecedented world tour in December 1907.

MISSION: IMPOSSIBLE

This trip was the brainchild of Teddy Roosevelt, towards the end of his second term as president. One of his purposes was to test the Navy's ships and train its men on the open seas. T. R. personally asked Archie and his colleague Edward Fullerton to participate as science advisers, traveling aboard the USS *Illinois*.

Roosevelt didn't reveal his entire plan from the start. Not until after the fleet departed from Virginia did its crews—and the public—learn that the ships would circle the world. Because the Panama Canal hadn't been completed yet, this meant traveling south all the way around the tip of South America, through the dangerous Straits of Magellan, then bearing north to California. From San Francisco the fleet would cross the Pacific, take the Suez Canal to the Mediterranean Sea, then ride the waves all the way across the Atlantic back home to Virginia.

Today, that may sound like a routine (if overblown) publicity stunt. But in 1907, it was a literally unheard-of feat. No naval fleet of any kind had ever accomplished such a deed. On top of that, steel battleships were still a novelty, and long-distance radio communication was in its infancy.

"[N]either the English nor the German authorities believed it possible to take a fleet of great battleships round the world. They did not believe that their own fleets could perform the feat, and still less did they believe that the American fleet could."

—Theodore Roosevelt,
An Autobiography (1913)

The battleship USS *Illinois*. During the Great White Fleet's world tour, this vessel was temporarily powered by the same technology as Boilerplate: Edward Fullerton's fuel cells.

Boilerplate at the stern of the USS *Illinois*, where the robot saved a sailor from being lost at sea.

"THEIR SPARKY LITTLE APPARATUS"

Archie and Fullerton's temporary home, the *Illinois*, was commanded by Captain John M. Bowyer. At first Bowyer did not welcome the distraction of having two civilians and a robot aboard, but his attitude eventually softened.

"Our good Captain Bowyer has at last divested himself of his prior disdain. My mechanical man proved his mettle by accelerating the coaling process, shoveling more coal than any five men. The men, pleased by the abbreviation of this arduous task, early on accepted Boilerplate into their ranks, even incorporating it into the skits they occasionally stage as shipboard entertainment. Meantime, Fullerton's experimental modifications have increased the vessel's efficiency and speed, and have thoroughly confounded the engineers to boot."

—Archibald Campion, letter to Mark Twain (July 25, 1908)

Archie's letters to Mark Twain make several references to Fullerton's "experiment" without fully explaining it. Many of Archie's letters to Nikola Tesla, which may have contained more technical detail, were

confiscated by the FBI along with other papers after Tesla's death. And official U.S. Navy records are silent on this point.

Based on anecdotal evidence, it appears that Fullerton, with Archie's help, modified one of the eight boilers aboard the *Illinois*. Instead of burning coal to heat the water, they used Fullerton's fuel cells to power a heating element that turned the water into steam. The experiment was a success, but the Navy decided the system was impractical for large-scale use because, ironically, it generated too much heat.

"We never did think those two know-it-alls knew a solitary thing about operating a battleship. And I wager we were in the right, because that was the last we saw of their sparky little apparatus in the Navy. That metal man with 'em, though, he was a marvel. He was a machine through and through, not a man inside a can, and don't let anyone tell you different."

—Julia Waissman, interview with J. H. Berryhill, *Men of the Great White Fleet* (Naval History Society, 1939)

A PARTY IN EVERY PORT

Boilerplate was a big attraction during port calls, as well as a big help to the fleet. In Brazil, the robot helped break up a bar brawl between U.S. sailors and local longshoremen, averting an international incident. After the fleet reached the West Coast, Boilerplate's notable activities include refereeing a boxing match in Los Angeles, erecting tents for sailors in San Francisco, and pulling a timber barge up the Willamette River in Oregon.

The fleet spent two months on the western U.S. seaboard, then continued west to Hawaii, where Archie talked Governor Sanford Dole into letting Boilerplate harvest fresh pineapple for the visiting seamen. The ships then crossed the Pacific to Australia, where a crowd of 250,000 greeted them with an eight-day celebration. By then, the crewmen were so partied out that Archie and Boilerplate found one of them asleep on a park bench under a homemade sign: *"I am delighted with the Australian people. I think your harbor the finest in the world. I am very tired and would like to sleep."*

THE LUCKY SALT

The Great White Fleet's voyage wasn't all parties and gunnery practice. From Australia, the fleet went to the Philippines. En route from there to Japan, in the South China Sea, it weathered one of the worst typhoons in

Shipboard cartoon by an unknown *Illinois* crew member.

forty years. The waves were so high that even these vast battleships were practically swallowed up by the troughs.

"All you could see of an entire battleship, when it was in trough, was the trunk of its mast above the wave tops. We very nearly lost a man in our squadron: One sailor was picked up and washed overboard by an enormous wave. Then that same wave carried him over to the Illinois and it threw him up in the air—and he was one lucky salt, because Campion's mechanical man happened to be on deck and snatched him from mid-air. I never witnessed the like before or since."

—Julia Waissman, interview with William Meagher, *Men of the Great White Fleet*

JAPAN GETS THE MESSAGE

Teddy Roosevelt had an ulterior purpose in mind when he first ordered the Atlantic Fleet to steam from Hampton Roads, Virginia, to San Francisco—to demonstrate to Japan that the United States could swiftly and easily relocate its naval squadrons. Japanese-American tensions were running high, partly as a result of the Roosevelt-brokered peace treaty that ended the Russo-Japanese War in 1905.

The Japanese were clearly impressed by the fleet when it arrived on their shores, welcoming its men with an elaborate series of parties, formal balls, and other celebrations. At least 50,000 people in Tokyo marched in a torchlight parade. During one event, a decorative arch caught fire and threatened to engulf a nearby Japanese flag. Boilerplate and several sailors raced over to rescue the flag just in time. They were feted as heroes and personally thanked by both Rear Admiral Sperry and Japanese Admiral Togo.

This postcard typifies the outpouring of sentiment that the fleet received around the globe.

The Great White Fleet, with running lights ablaze, was a unique spectacle for observers on shore.

"SPEAK SOFTLY AND CARRY A BIG STICK"

After visiting several other countries and traversing the Mediterranean Sea, the Great White Fleet began the long final leg of its around-the-world journey, arriving back in Virginia on February 22, 1909. Thanks to Roosevelt's gumption, the fleet's officers and men got a good dose of at-sea training and a chance to discover any flaws in ship design. After the voyage, the fleet commanders, Archie, and Fullerton made recommendations that produced significant technological improvements in battleships.

A decade earlier, the United States had made its first mark as a world power by winning a naval victory in the Spanish-American War, with only four first-class battleships. Now it had twenty brand-new vessels of the most modern type. When T. R. left office a few weeks after the Great White Fleet returned home, he was satisfied that he had helped his nation step up into the big leagues—with a little help from Archie and Boilerplate.

"In my own judgment the most important service that I rendered to peace was the voyage of the battle-fleet around the world."

—Theodore Roosevelt, *An Autobiography*

BOXING DAY

In 1910, Archie and his Mechanical Marvel met champion boxer Jack Johnson, who was intrigued by the possibility of using Boilerplate as a sparring partner. Johnson was the first black World Heavyweight Boxing Champion, from 1908 to 1915. He fought more than a hundred matches, knocking out his opponents in nearly half of them. This publicity still was taken at his training camp outside Reno, Nevada, a few months before the *Fight of the Century* between Johnson and James J. Jeffries, aka the *Great White Hope*.

Boilerplate went a few rounds with the Champ. The only problem was, Boilerplate exhibited no recoil from body blows—the robot didn't budge, no matter how hard Johnson hit it. The full, bone-jarring impact of every pile-driver punch was channeled back into Johnson's hands and arms, instead of being partially absorbed by his opponent. He decided that sparring with a metal man wasn't such a clever idea after all.

Back then, practically every white American male was a boxing fan. Unfortunately, a lot of them didn't look kindly on the championship belt being worn by a black man. And so Johnson, though he became the first black celebrity in U.S. history, discovered that fame without respect is a heavy burden. His reign as world champion was ended by Jess Willard, in a fight that many now believe was fixed.

"You would be appalled, as am I, by the many indignities, and the overt contempt, visited upon Mr. Johnson by whites. I am ashamed to be confronted with the knowledge that so many of my own race have so little regard for what lies behind a dusky visage. They treat this fine, strong, intelligent man as one would a caged beast—alluring yet deadly, prone to eating its keepers if unrestrained—and they would deny to their last breath that his nobility and power are worthy of emulation.

"Mr. Johnson, for his part, appears to enjoy the company of my mechanical man. Being utterly lacking in emotion, the automaton is similarly lacking in prejudice, which sets him at ease. I believe that is a rare pleasure for this remarkable fighter."

—Archibald Campion, letter to Lily Campion
(February 11, 1910)

Jack Johnson poses with sparring partner, May 1910. Lily Campion is in the background.

Girls in a textile mill with Boilerplate. Lewis Hine's photographs of working kids were instrumental in the eventual outlawing of child labor.

The incomparable Winsor McCay occasionally drew political cartoons on subjects that were important to him, such as child labor.

CHILDHOOD'S END

In 1911, Archie Campion got an up-close look at one of industrial America's most shocking secrets: the harsh life of child workers. Tragically, their numbers swelled during the nineteenth century as employers sought new sources of cheap, easily managed labor.

Archie and Boilerplate traveled for several months with photographer Lewis Hine, who worked for the National Child Labor Committee (NCLC). Hine spent a decade documenting the hazards and abuses endured by children as young as five years old in canneries, textile mills, coal mines, cotton fields, meatpacking houses, glass factories, sweatshops, and street trades. He often had to use a pretext to gain entry to these workplaces and photograph the children covertly, because employers didn't want his type of publicity.

"There is work that profits children, and there is work that brings profit only to employers. The object of employing children is not to train them, but to get high profits from their work."
—Lewis Hine (1908)

Lily Campion and her friend Jane Addams had told Archie how rough things were for these kids, but he couldn't quite believe it until he saw their plight himself.

He saw children who got up before dawn, or worked the night shift, doing twelve to fourteen hours of grueling labor in life-threatening conditions, six days a week.

Many child workers were helping their families eke out a hardscrabble living. Others were barely surviving on the streets as orphans. With no time or money for school, most grew up illiterate, unable to even sign their own names. Addams thought Boilerplate offered at least a partial solution to the problem.

"How much of this drudgery could instead be accomplished by a tireless machine, such that the children might remain in school and better their lot? Their education would be of far greater benefit to the commonweal than is their mindless subjugation."
—Jane Addams, "The Objective Value of a Social Settlement" (1893)

Hine's *photo-stories*, as he called them, aroused widespread calls for change. Some states already had labor laws on the books that were supposed to protect children, but the laws either weren't enforced or were full of business-friendly loopholes. Several attempts to safeguard child workers through federal legislation failed or were struck down by the U.S. Supreme Court.

The NCLC kept trying, with Archie and Lily's help. At last, in 1938 President Franklin Roosevelt signed into law the Fair Labor Standards Act (FLSA). The FLSA banned *"oppressive child labor,"* set a minimum hourly wage for the first time, and limited the maximum workweek to forty-four hours.

The NCLC still pursues its mission of preventing the exploitation of children in the labor market. Each year, it gives out an award in Lewis Hine's name.

Young coal miners pose with Boilerplate. This photo, taken by the famed Lewis Hine, was intended to demonstrate how a robot could replace a dozen or more boys in mining operations. Campion was willing to bend his policy on using Boilerplate as a laborer, if it meant an end to an immoral business practice.

"Seldom have I seen true fury burning in my brother's eyes. Upon returning from his tour with Mr. Hine, Archie was positively aflame with anger. Though we do not speak of it, I know that he and I feel a kinship with these children, having been orphaned ourselves. We are fortunate that we were never reduced to such piteous desperation as these waifs who spill their blood that we may have fine gloves and warm parlors."

—Lily Campion, letter to Carrie Chapman Catt (September 23, 1911)

CHAPTER 4

TALES OF A METAL DOUGHBOY

—⁓— *or* —⁓—

BOILERPLATE IN COMBAT

Although Archie Campion never realized his dream of replacing human soldiers with robots, Boilerplate amassed an impressive military record in a relatively short time. Between 1898 and 1918, the mechanical soldier served on three continents with famous commanders such as Teddy Roosevelt, Black Jack Pershing, and Lawrence of Arabia.

Boilerplate kitted out for the Cuban campaign, San Juan Heights, July 1898.

THE SPANISH-AMERICAN WAR

As soon as the United States declared war on Spain in April 1898, Archie saw his opportunity to arrange a battlefield demonstration of his creation's combat capabilities. He rushed back from the Klondike in hopes of joining the first American war to come along since he'd built Boilerplate.

END OF EMPIRE

Even before the war began, the once mighty Spanish empire was in its twilight, left with only a few scattered colonies that it had ruled since the sixteenth century. It teetered on the brink of civil war at home and faced incessant rebellions in both Cuba and the Philippines.

After losing control over parts of Cuba, Spain cracked down on the rest of the country in 1896. The U.S. was leaning toward intervening to support the Cuban rebels. Public outrage in the States was rising fast, fueled in part by newspaper publishers such as William Randolph Hearst and Joseph Pulitzer, who used tales of brutality in Cuba to sell papers in New York.

"REMEMBER THE *MAINE!*"

On February 15, 1898, the battleship USS *Maine* exploded and sank in Havana harbor. The ship's own ammunition magazine blew up, set off by a fire in the adjacent coal bunker. The Navy's investigators at the time, though, decided that the explosion was caused by a mine of unknown origin. Overwrought reports blamed the Spanish, and Hearst's paper the *New York Morning Journal* went so far as to print a fake Spanish telegram about the *Maine*. America got swept up in the rush to war.

President McKinley at first opposed U.S. intervention in Cuba, but powerful factions were pushing for it. One such faction, centered around Teddy Roosevelt, met for lunches at the Metropolitan Club in Washington, D.C. George Dewey, Henry Cabot Lodge, Alfred Mahan, and other prominent men were connected to T. R.'s group. They favored an expansionist foreign policy and wanted to claim more territory, as the European imperial powers had done. With the American frontier officially closed, the next frontier lay overseas.

Roosevelt was then Assistant Secretary of the Navy. He knew that the Spanish-controlled Philippine Islands were another likely theater of war. He ordered Commodore George Dewey to prepare the Navy's Asiatic Squadron to attack the Philippines in case war broke out between the U.S. and Spain.

The USS *Maine* explodes in Havana harbor, touching off the Spanish-American War.

By ratcheting up international tensions in the Pacific, Roosevelt made the war practically inevitable.

ROUGH RIDERS AT THE READY

In late April, the United States issued a formal declaration of war against Spain. President McKinley called for 125,000 volunteers to join the U.S. military. The next month, Roosevelt resigned from his Navy position so he could form the 1st Volunteer Cavalry Regiment to fight the Spanish in Cuba. Many of the new volunteers had no combat experience and were hurriedly trained en route to their departure point in Tampa, Florida.

Archie, aware of T. R.'s fascination with cutting-edge technology, wired him to ask if Boilerplate could join Roosevelt's unit, the Rough Riders. The offer was gladly accepted. Soon Archie and Boilerplate were with Roosevelt on a transport ship bound for Cuba. The Spanish-American War was under way.

A VERDANT BATTLEFIELD

On June 22, 1898, U.S. forces—including Archie and Boilerplate—landed without opposition at Daiquiri in Cuba. The next day, they advanced to the nearby town of Siboney and established a supply base. Their goal was to make their way west and north up the coast, then take Santiago, Cuba's capital and the last Spanish stronghold. Colonel Leonard Wood led the Rough Riders, with Roosevelt as his second in command. Archie stayed behind in the relative safety of Siboney.

Cuban rebels reported seeing Spanish entrenchments only a few thousand yards to the northwest, at Las Guásimas. Wood ordered a probe of the Spanish position. And so, on June 24, Boilerplate engaged in combat for the first time in the five years since the robot had been constructed for that very purpose.

Underwood & Underwood, Publishers
New York, London, Toronto-Canada, Ottawa-Kansas.

Works and Studios
Arlington, N.J. Littleton, N.H. Washington, D.C.

Colonel Teddy Roosevelt and Boilerplate in Tampa, Florida, just before their departure for Cuba during the Spanish-American War.

T. R. was in the left column of the American advance. Tromping through the jungle alongside him were Boilerplate and noted journalist Edward Marshall of the *New York Journal*, each armed with the latest Kraig rifles. The Americans took fire from the Spanish forces but managed to drive them back. Marshall and several Rough Riders were wounded during a series of skirmishes. Near the jungle's edge, the Spaniards took refuge in a blockhouse surrounded by a clearing.

Roosevelt suspected that Boilerplate might have a dramatic effect on demoralized enemy soldiers. He ordered the mechanical man to advance on the blockhouse. The remaining Spanish troops first watched in disbelief as their bullets ricocheted off Boilerplate's metal torso,

then turned and fled toward Santiago. Only the Spanish defenses at San Juan Heights now stood between the Americans and Cuba's capital.

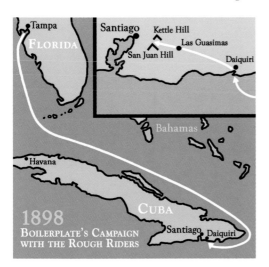

Tampa
FLORIDA
Santiago
Kettle Hill
Las Guasimas
San Juan Hill
Daiquiri
Bahamas
Havana
CUBA
1898
BOILERPLATE'S CAMPAIGN WITH THE ROUGH RIDERS
Santiago   Daiquiri

Boilerplate, Teddy Roosevelt, and journalist Edward Marshall, moments before being fired on by Spaniards in the robot's first combat experience.

"MY MECHANICAL MULE"

On July 1, U.S. forces assaulted the two hills at San Juan Heights—Kettle Hill and San Juan Hill—in a disorganized but determined charge. Lieutenant John "Black Jack" Pershing led the 10th Cavalry, while

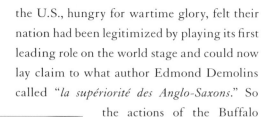

Kettle Hill

Barbed wire

Spanish defenses

San Juan Hill

Roosevelt & Rough Riders

BOILERPLATE'S CHARGE

Pershing & Buffalo Soldiers

Spanish defenses

Regular infantry & cavalry

Press corps

Observation balloon

U.S. FORCES

Barbed wire

JULY 1 1898

Roosevelt led the Rough Riders. Roosevelt described it as "*my crowded hour*" and wrote:

"*I galloped toward the hill, passing the shouting, cheering, firing men, and went up the lane, splashing through a small stream; when I got abreast of the ranch buildings on the top of Kettle Hill, I turned and went up the slope. Being on horseback, I was of course able to get ahead of the men on foot, excepting my mechanical 'mule,' who had run ahead very fast in order to get better shots at the Spaniards, who were now running out of the ranch buildings.*"

—Col. Theodore Roosevelt, *The Rough Riders* (1899)

The *mechanical mule* was, of course, Boilerplate. Roosevelt acknowledged Boilerplate's contribution and even admitted that the first troops up the hill were from the all-black 9th and 10th Cavalry, popularly known as the *Buffalo Soldiers*. A guidon-bearer of the 10th Cavalry was the first to plant an American standard on Kettle Hill.

Nevertheless, T. R. didn't hesitate to take most of the credit for winning this crucial battle. The press shone the spotlight on him and romanticized the Rough Riders. Many in

the U.S., hungry for wartime glory, felt their nation had been legitimized by playing its first leading role on the world stage and could now lay claim to what author Edmond Demolins called "*la supériorité des Anglo-Saxons.*" So the actions of the Buffalo Soldiers and Boilerplate were all but ignored, in favor of the Rough Riders story.

Two days after that famous charge up San Juan Heights, the Spanish fleet was decimated while trying to break through the American naval blockade of Santiago's harbor. General José Toral surrendered the capital on July 17, 1898. The following month, Boilerplate shipped back to the States with the Rough Riders.

INSTANT EMPIRE

The United States and Spain signed a final peace treaty in Paris on December 10, 1898. Spain granted nominal independence to Cuba, but the U.S. continued to occupy and/or control the former colony for decades. The American military base at Guantánamo in Cuba remains active today.

Spain ceded control of the Philippines, Guam, and Puerto Rico to the United States, in exchange for $20 million. Guam and Puerto Rico are still U.S. territories. The fiftieth state was also acquired during the war: In July 1898, the United States annexed Hawaii, which wasn't a Spanish possession but was strategically situated between California naval bases and the Philippines.

With its victory in the Spanish-American War, the United States—unified against a common foe for the first time since the divisive American Civil War—became a world power engaged in empire-building.

PION'S MECHANICAL MARVEL

HE CHARGE OF SAN JUAN HILL
N AND COL. ROOSEVELT, LEADING THE FAMOUS "ROUGH RIDERS" TO VICTORY.

It marked a turning point for Archie, too, as Boilerplate's first wartime combat mission.

"My mechanical soldier performed admirably indeed, winning favor with officers and enlisted men, too. Colonel Roosevelt's vigorous praise in particular gives me cause to believe that our military may adopt my proposed means of preventing the deaths of men in battle."

—Archibald Campion, letter to Frank Reade, Jr. (August 3, 1898)

"It has been a splendid little war, begun with the highest motives, carried on with magnificent intelligence and spirit, favored by that Fortune which loves the brave."

—Ambassador John Hay, letter to Col. Theodore Roosevelt (July 27, 1898)

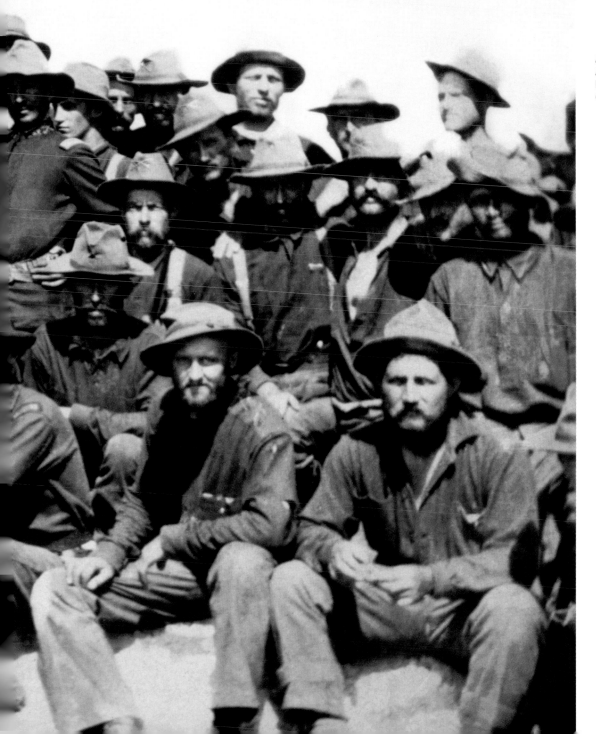

Boilerplate with the Rough Riders atop San Juan Hill in Cuba, after their famous charge of July 1, 1898.

A medal given by Roosevelt to Archie Campion, in recognition of Boilerplate's service during the Cuban campaign.

THE PHILIPPINE-AMERICAN WAR

While Boilerplate and Col. Teddy Roosevelt were charging up San Juan Heights in Cuba, American armed forces were also attacking the Spanish thousands of miles away in Manila, capital of the Philippine Islands. Archie Campion didn't know it yet, but the Philippines would be his robot's next battleground.

Cartoon criticizing the new U.S. holdings as imperialist.

MEET THE NEW BOSS

Like Cuba, the Philippines had been under Spanish rule for centuries and were struggling to achieve independence. At the end of 1897, Spain quashed the latest Filipino uprising and banished General Emilio Aguinaldo, one of the rebel leaders. Only a few months later, the U.S. brought Aguinaldo back to the Philippines and supplied him with more than 2,000 rifles so he could organize Filipino fighters to help oust the Spanish.

In June 1898, during the Spanish-American War, Aguinaldo announced that he had formed a new, independent Philippine national government. But the Spanish ignored him. They surrendered Manila on August 13 to the Americans—who occupied the city, cordoned it off, and prohibited Filipino *insurrectos* from entering. The Philippines became U.S. property under the Treaty of Paris in December.

"[T]he mission of the United States is one of BENEVOLENT ASSIMILATION, substituting the mild sway of justice and right for arbitrary rule. In the fulfillment of this high mission . . . there must be sedulously maintained the strong arm of authority, to repress disturbance

Filipino infantry during the early phase of the war, wearing uniforms with white-duck waistcoats and straw hats. Later, after turning to guerrilla tactics, they also switched to less formal attire.

General Emilio Aguinaldo, leader of the Philippine rebellion against Spanish rule and U.S. occupation.

and to overcome all obstacles to the bestowal of the blessings of good and stable government upon the people of the Philippine Islands under the free flag of the United States."

—President William McKinley, "Benevolent Assimilation Proclamation" (December 21, 1898)

SOUTH PACIFIC

Meanwhile, T. R. and the Rough Riders had returned to the States from Cuba and were starting a six-week quarantine on Long Island, New York. There was some debate about whether Boilerplate should be quarantined, too, but Archie successfully argued that a thorough cleaning would be enough to disinfect the mechanical man.

At Roosevelt's recommendation, Boilerplate was soon redeployed to Manila. Archie and Lily Campion journeyed to Hong Kong with the robot. There they parted ways, Lily heading for Peking to visit a friend, Archie and Boilerplate traveling southeast to the Philippines.

On January 1, 1899, not long before the professor and his automaton arrived in Manila, Aguinaldo was proclaimed president of the Philippine Republic. The U.S. refused to recognize the new nation. The armed standoff around Manila grew edgier by the day. When an American soldier fired the first shot on February 4, the Philippine-American War—usually called the *Philippine insurrection* in the United States—started with a bang.

↑ A field telegraph office near Poco Bridge, during a battle on February 5, 1899. Lt. Gibbs of the Volunteer Signal Corps prepares to dispatch Boilerplate on a communications mission. Wearing a wire-spool backpack as shown here, the metal soldier would run from one position to another, stringing telegraph line as it went. An ideal role for the robot, as it was impervious to gunfire.

↓ Downtown Manila on the Philippine island of Luzon, 1899.

"About eight o'clock, Miller and I were cautiously pacing our district. We came to a fence and were trying to see what the Filipinos were up to. Then a red lantern flashed a signal from blockhouse number 7. We had never seen such a sign used before. In a moment, something rose up slowly in front of us. It was a Filipino. I yelled 'Halt!' and made it pretty loud. I challenged him with another loud 'halt!' Then he shouted 'halto!' to me. Well, I thought the best thing to do was to shoot him. He dropped. If I didn't kill him, I guess he died of fright."

—Pvt. William W. Grayson, describing the first shot in the Philippine-American War

BLACK JACK AND THE MECHANICAL SAPPER

Archie stayed in Manila while Boilerplate went into the field. The robot was assigned to tasks such as laying communication wires, guarding Manila's water supply, digging trenches, and hauling heavy loads.

"It would seem that the military leaders here suffer from a fatal failure of imagination. They do not yet appreciate the intended purpose of my mechanical soldier, despite its recent success in Cuba. Rather than serving in the stead of men on the battle field, my automaton has been assigned to 'sapper' duties—in essence, simple manual labor."

—Archibald Campion, letter to Frank Reade, Jr. (April 25, 1899)

⬆ Boilerplate with the 20th Kansas on February 8, 1899.

1 The CO of Number 2 Blockhouse inspects Boilerplate. Many such outposts surrounded Manila, just outside the suburbs. Over the course of the Spanish-American and Philippine-American wars, the blockhouses were used by the Spanish against Philippine and American forces, then by Philippine rebels against Americans and vice versa.

2 Boilerplate does sentry duty next to guns used by the Utah Light Battery during an engagement at *el Deposito*, the Manila waterworks, February 26, 1899. The robot often served as a sentry, because there was no danger of it falling asleep or being felled by an enemy sniper.

3 Another menial task for the metal soldier: Boilerplate positions artillery for the 20th Kansas Regiment.

4 Boilerplate helps the 20th Kansas Regiment dig trenches just before the battle at Caloocan, February 10, 1899. Enemy snipers in the distant tree lines sporadically harassed U.S. positions.

The railroad depot at Malolos, March 1899. The American officers with Boilerplate are Generals Harrison Otis, Arthur MacArthur, and Irving Hale. This photo was taken about a half hour after the retreat of Gen. Aguinaldo and his rebel forces.

"Talk about war being 'hell,' this war beats the hottest estimate ever made of that locality. Caloocan was supposed to contain seventeen thousand inhabitants. The Twentieth Kansas swept through it, and now Caloocan contains not one living native. Of the buildings, the battered walls of the great church and dismal prison alone remain. The village of Maypaja, where our first fight occurred on the night of the fourth, had 5,000 people on that day—now not one stone remains upon top of another. You can only faintly imagine this terrible scene of desolation. War is worse than hell."
—Capt. David Stewart Elliott, 20th Kansas Regiment (1899)

➡ Boilerplate helps carry a litter of wounded men from the 20th Kansas Regiment, returning from a skirmish near the Pasig River southeast of Manila.

⬅ General Charles King and his staff with Boilerplate, outside the former residence of Gen. Luna. During the war, Spanish haciendas in the Philippines were partially stripped of their ornate, valuable contents by departing owners, then further looted by Philippine rebels, and finally emptied out— and sometimes destroyed—by the U.S. military.

"The building had been taken possession of by a United States officer, and he looted it to a finish. He was half drunk, and every time he saw me looking at anything he would say, 'Tennessee, do you like that? Well, put it in your pocket.' The contents of every drawer had been emptied on the floor. You have no idea what a mania for destruction the average man has when the fear of the law is removed. I have seen them— old sober businessmen too— knock chandeliers and plate-glass mirrors to pieces just because they couldn't carry it off. It is such a pity."
—D. M. Mickle, Tennessee Regiment

The closest Boilerplate got to serving as a combat soldier in the Philippines was a few reconnaissance missions for Bvt. Maj. John "Black Jack" Pershing, who arrived in August 1899. Pershing recognized the metal soldier's inherent value for high-risk duty on the front lines, where fatalities were commonplace.

AN UGLY TURN

The Filipino Army of Liberation fought a series of losing battles using conventional tactics until late 1899, when it broke up into smaller units and switched to guerrilla strategies. On the American side, the McKinley administration's plans for the Philippines were somewhat haphazard, so the War Department failed to give clear or consistent direction. Officers in the field often made tactical decisions on the fly, based on incomplete or flat-out wrong information. U.S. troops knew next to nothing about the Philippines' cultures, languages, or geography.

Under such circumstances, the war predictably devolved into a quagmire. In response to Filipino guerrilla attacks and supposed civilian collusion, the American occupying forces started burning entire towns, looting haciendas, and rounding up villagers into concentration camps.

HIT HIM HARD!

PRESIDENT McKinley—"Mosquitoes seem to be worse here in the Philippines than they were in Cuba."

McKinley regarding Aguinaldo as a mere pest.

Filipino soldiers, wounded while fighting for their country's freedom from foreign rule, await evacuation to a medical facility. The American press referred to them as *insurgents*.

The savagery escalated on both sides. Casualties were, however, much higher on the Filipino side, numbering in the hundreds of thousands.

"Perhaps I should have heeded your sage advice and eschewed any involvement in this particular war. I am of two minds on it. Undeniably the war's conduct has grown vicious, and it is all for the sake of subduing a people who desire to achieve self-governance. An ignominious casus belli, to be sure.

"Yet such wars will be waged with no regard whatsoever for your opinion or mine, so why should not my mechanical man do its part to prevent further squandering of human life? I am gratified if my invention has preserved even one life that would otherwise have been sacrificed, though I maintain it would have preserved many more had it been put to service in the infantry."

—Archibald Campion, letter to Mark Twain (July 9, 1900)

MISSION ACCOMPLISHED

The Americans captured Emilio Aguinaldo on March 23, 1901, more than two years after the Philippine-American War began. By then, President McKinley had been re-elected in the States, with Teddy Roosevelt as his vice president. T. R. ascended to the presidency when McKinley was assassinated in September of that same year.

On July 4, 1902, Roosevelt announced that the Philippine insurrection had officially ended. In reality, sporadic fighting persisted for at least a decade.

The Philippine Islands were granted limited autonomy as a commonwealth in 1935, but were then invaded and occupied by Japan during World War II. On July 4, 1946, the Philippines at last gained full independence from the United States.

Boilerplate missed both the official and the unofficial end of the Philippine-American conflict. In June 1900, Archie received word that the foreign embassies in Peking, where Lily was staying, were under attack by Chinese nationalists. Archie immediately recalled Boilerplate from the field, and soon they were en route to Peking—to rescue Lily from the Boxer Rebellion.

REBEL WITH A CAUSE

For a few weeks in early 1900, Boilerplate was attached to a special scouting party. Their object: Capture former Cpl. David Fagen, a U.S. Army defector who was fast turning into one of the Philippine rebels' best guerilla commanders.

David Fagen began the war as a U.S. Army corporal and ended it as a Philippine rebel general.

Fagen had served honorably with the 24th Regiment in Cuba. In the Philippines, his regiment saw action in brutal battles against the *insurrectos* in central Luzon, the largest of the islands. But Fagen, who was black, encountered problems with his superiors there. They reportedly picked on him and forced him to do *"all sorts of dirty jobs."*

He started to sympathize with the Filipino cause. On November 17, 1899, with help from a rebel officer, Fagen slipped out of his barracks and rode away into the night. Over the next year, he clashed with American troops at least eight times and became legendary for his ability to evade capture. Even the *New York Times* reported on his exploits.

Boilerplate's party located one of "General" Fagen's abandoned camps, but not the man himself. In 1901 the $1,000 bounty on his head was awarded to a local hunter who gave the Army a severed head that he claimed was Fagen's. However, the head was never conclusively identified, and Army records refer to the incident as *"the supposed killing of David Fagen."*

At the time, popular opinion among the natives held that Fagen had fabricated his own murder. Some say he lived out his days peacefully in a mountain village with his Filipina wife.

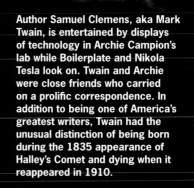

Author Samuel Clemens, aka Mark Twain, is entertained by displays of technology in Archie Campion's lab while Boilerplate and Nikola Tesla look on. Twain and Archie were close friends who carried on a prolific correspondence. In addition to being one of America's greatest writers, Twain had the unusual distinction of being born during the 1835 appearance of Halley's Comet and dying when it reappeared in 1910.

A LEAGUE FOR JUSTICE

Many Americans believed their government had acted with needless belligerence and was now betraying its own origins by suppressing the independence movement in the Philippines. A group of prominent citizens—including Jane Addams, Mark Twain, Andrew Carnegie, and former President Grover Cleveland—formed the Anti-Imperialist League and agitated for U.S. withdrawal from the Philippines.

Archie's friend Twain, who was living in England, at first supported the Spanish-American War because he thought its main goal was to free Cuba. But once he saw the Philippine-American War dragging on, he realized that the United States was becoming exactly what it had fought its own war of independence against: an imperial power.

"I have thought some more, since then, and I have read carefully the Treaty of Paris, and I have seen that we do not intend to free, but to subjugate the people of the Philippines. We have gone there to conquer, not to redeem.

"It should, it seems to me, be our pleasure and duty to make those people free, and let them deal with their own domestic questions in their own way. And so I am an anti-imperialist. I am opposed to having the eagle put its talons on any other land."

—Mark Twain, "An Anti-Imperialist," *New York Herald* (October 15, 1900)

"Our fathers, who won the Revolution and who framed the Constitution . . . did not disdain to study ancient history. They knew what caused the downfall of the mighty Roman Republic. They read . . . the history of the freedom, the decay, and the enslavement of Greece . . . They learned from her that while there is little else a democracy cannot accomplish, it cannot rule over vassal states of subject peoples without bringing the elements of death into its own constitution.

"There are two lessons our fathers learned from the history of Greece which they hoped their children would remember—the danger of disunion . . . and lust of empire."

—Sen. George Frisbie Hoar (R-Mass.), address to the Senate (January 8, 1899)

THE BOXER REBELLION

Starting in late June 1900, the foreign embassies in Peking (now Beijing), China, were besieged by the Chinese. Thousands of foreigners—among them Lily Campion—were trapped in the walled Legation Quarter inside the city, their fate unknown. Archie and Boilerplate sailed from the Philippines for Taku, China, to join the army of the Eight-Nation Alliance and save Lily.

"My mechanical soldier and I shall join the Allied forces at Tien Tsin in time to march on Peking. As to Lily's fate, I fear the worst yet hope for the best. If there is the slightest chance that she still lives, I must do all within my power to secure her safety.

"Should we meet our end, you must make every effort to reclaim Boilerplate on my behalf and to prevent my inventions from being exploited for crass or deleterious ends. In the event of my death and my sister's, I hereby expressly bequeath to you my laboratory and all of its contents, my mechanical man, and my patents and all agreements associated therewith. I confer upon you a power of attorney in perpetuity for purposes of executing this bequest."

—Archibald Campion, letter to Edward Fullerton (July 16, 1900)

Boilerplate assists the 14th Regiment's Easy Company as they scale the Peking city wall near Tung Pien gate, August 14, 1900. The military operation that defeated the Boxer Rebellion was a unique collaboration among eight nations. This victorious scene was repeated at other parts of the wall by soldiers from countries such as France and Japan. Each nation has immortalized the historic assault in illustrations depicting its own men triumphantly raising a flag at the top of the wall.

Westerners called these Chinese nationalists *Boxers* because of their kung-fu fighting style, which was not well known outside Asia at the time. The Boxers' goal was to end foreign influence over their country.

SPHERES OF INFLUENCE

The nineteenth century was the beginning of the end for imperial China. The Qing dynasty, the last in the country's long history, was losing power and in 1895 suffered an embarrassing defeat by Japan in the Sino-Japanese War.

Foreign nations moved in and carved up parts of China, staking out *spheres of influence* in which they held exclusive railway, mining, and other commercial rights. The Russians took control of Port Arthur (Lüshun), for

Spheres of
Influence
1900

MONGOLIA   MANCHURIA

CHINA   Peking ●

Shanghai ●

Hong Kong ●

PACIFIC
OCEAN

RUSSIA
JAPAN
BRITAIN
FRANCE
GERMANY

example, and the British got Hong Kong. China was also forced to sign a series of unequal treaties granting special rights to foreigners and opening its waterways to outside commerce and warships.

The Chinese resented these usurpations. As antiforeigner sentiment gained steam in China, secretive organizations grew more influential. One such group was the *I Ho Ch'uan*—variously translated as *Righteous Harmony Society*, *Righteous Harmonious Fists*, or *Fists of Righteous Harmony*—otherwise known as the *Boxers*, who considered foreign influence literally evil.

THE SIEGE OF PEKING

After traveling to Hong Kong with Archie in 1899, Lily went north to visit her friend Simone Pichon, sister of French diplomat Stéphen Pichon, at the Legation Quarter in Peking. It was not a good time to drop by.

Backed by tacit support from the Dowager Empress Tzu Hsi, who secretly hoped to expel the nettlesome Western nations from China, the Boxer movement ran wild. Its adherents killed foreigners and Chinese Christian converts, destroyed railroads, and cut telegraph lines.

In June 1900, the Chinese government issued a thinly veiled demand that all foreigners leave Peking. When that edict was ignored, China laid siege to the Legation Quarter and declared war on the Eight-Nation Alliance of Austria-Hungary, France, Germany, Great Britain, Italy, Japan, Russia, and the United States. Chinese imperial troops started openly collaborating with the Boxers.

Lily, Simone, and thousands of others were surrounded by hostile forces, cut off from the outside world. With only a few hundred troops to defend them, and no relief in sight, they did their best to fortify the Legation Quarter. For fifty-five long days, they hunkered down behind makeshift barricades and withstood shelling, mines, machine guns, arson, and infantry assaults.

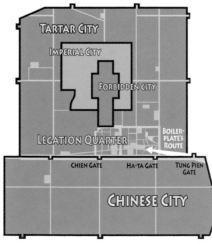

Boilerplate plows through Boxers, ahead of Easy Company, in an effort to rescue Lily from Peking's embassy district. Many accounts describe the robot using its rifle as a quarterstaff in combat, and discharging the weapon only for covering fire. It is possible that Boilerplate never actually killed anyone, thus fulfilling—in an unexpected way—Campion's original intent that his invention would prevent men from dying in international conflicts.

THE ALLIES ADVANCE

Meanwhile, Archie and Boilerplate made their way to Tien Tsin, where they joined a multinational relief expedition of about 20,000 troops. An earlier rescue effort spearheaded by British Vice Admiral Edward Seymour had already tried to reach Peking, only to be beaten back and itself require rescue by the larger army.

On August 4, 1900, the new expedition set out for Peking, Boilerplate marching with the U.S. Army's 14th Infantry regiment. Over the next eight days, the Allied forces took one town after another, routing the Chinese army, until they reached Tung Chow (Tongzhou District). From there, they planned to launch a coordinated attack on Peking. Archie still held out hope that Lily was alive.

"I am stricken with dread by even a passing thought of losing her . . . such treacherous thoughts refuse to be banished."

—Archibald Campion, letter to Edward Fullerton (July 16, 1900)

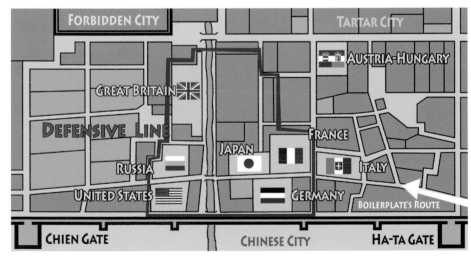

FORBIDDEN CITY | TARTAR CITY

AUSTRIA-HUNGARY

GREAT BRITAIN

DEFENSIVE LINE

FRANCE

JAPAN

RUSSIA | ITALY

UNITED STATES | GERMANY

BOILERPLATE'S ROUTE

CHIEN GATE | CHINESE CITY | HA-TA GATE

ASSAULT ON THE WALLED CITY

At dawn on August 14, Archie awoke to discover that the Russians had launched their assault prematurely, in a mad dash to be first in Peking. Worse, the Russians were attacking the Americans' designated target: Tung Pien gate. Forced to improvise, the U.S. commanders decided to find a way to get over the wall in between the well-defended gates.

With Boilerplate's able assistance, a young bugler from the 14th Infantry, Calvin Titus, managed to scale the wall. He found it unmanned, and a small contingent of his comrades quickly used a rope and a makeshift ladder to join him. They then cleared the way for the Russians by outflanking and driving off the Chinese who were defending Tung Pien gate.

As Russian and American soldiers spilled into the streets of Peking, Boilerplate and Archie made a beeline for the Legation Quarter. They got there just in time to help the British break in via a sluice gate on the Imperial Canal and, at last, end the siege. The next day, the Dowager Empress fled Peking. Boilerplate hoisted Archie up onto his shoulders and headed for the French legation.

"That Professor Campion was an odd duck, mind you. He rode into the Foreign Quarter perched atop his mechanical man, bobbing along above the fray. Comical a sight though they was, the iron soldier did cut a sure swath through enemy forces, and we gratefully followed in its wake."

—Matthew Page, interview with Cpl. Ian Tice, *The China Relief Expedition of 1900* (Boundary House, 1920)

THE CARVING KNIFE BRIGADE

Inside the Legation Quarter, Archie's heart sank when he saw that the French legation, where Lily had been staying, lay partially in ruins. But he soon learned that many foreigners had taken refuge in the British legation—and that's where he found Lily, leading a brigade of women armed with carving knives.

Although Archie and Lily had both seen quite enough of China, it wasn't yet safe to leave Peking. They had to wait until October, when the Boxer uprising was quelled in surrounding areas, to depart with Boilerplate. Archie's friend Frank Reade Jr. met the Campions at Taku and spirited them away in his airship.

"What joy suffused me at the sight of Frank's airship! After so many months of hostilities, I can scarcely wait to settle in to friendly environs. Now we shall have a well-deserved rest, aloft in the clouds where peace reigns. We are bound for Australia to greet the new century and the new commonwealth all at once. May the twentieth century be a gentler age than the one we bid farewell."

—Lily Campion, letter to Carrie Chapman Catt (November 7, 1900)

↑ Boilerplate atop the Peking wall, a few days after the Allies took the city.

➡ Shortly after Boilerplate helped relieve the besieged foreign legations in Peking, officers of the Eight-Nation Alliance gather in the courtyard of the British embassy. The Austro-Hungarian, German, and American inspect Boilerplate, while the British, Japanese, Russian, and Italian officers converse. For reasons unkown, there is no French officer pictured.

Lily Campion organized the wives of the various ambassadors hiding in the British compound, to help defend it.

382 Boilerplate on top of Southern Gate, Peking, China.

CHINA CAPITULATES

The Dowager Empress fled Peking the day after its walls were breached. A defeated China acceded to the Allies' "suggestions"—such as monetary reparations, political reforms, foreign military control, and mining concessions—and in September 1901 signed yet another unequal treaty, the Boxer Protocol. Only a decade later, the Qing dynasty was overthrown during the Xinhai Revolution, and the monarchy was supplanted by the Republic of China.

The Eight-Nation Alliance was a unique coalition, never to be repeated. In the decades to follow, various combinations of the former allies squared off against each other in military, economic, and ideological battles.

It was one such conflict, the Russo-Japanese War, that unexpectedly trapped Archie and Boilerplate several years later in another besieged Asian city: Port Arthur, Manchuria.

229. Bridge at Kanuyabashi, Near Kyoto, Japan.

Boilerplate was the first robot to walk on Japanese soil, in 1903.

THE RUSSO-JAPANESE WAR

In February 1904, long-simmering rivalry between Japan and Russia boiled over into a war of unprecedented scale—one that threatened to engulf Europe—and Archie Campion got caught smack in the middle of it.

THE GREAT BEAR MOVES EAST

As imperial China's strength faded and Japan rapidly modernized itself, Japan and Russia became the dominant powers in Asia. These three nations vied for control of Korea and Manchuria, which lie between Russia and Japan.

The balance of power shifted many times during the latter nineteenth century. Japan briefly controlled the strategically located Port Arthur in Manchuria, but was forced to give it up in 1895. Russia took over the Port Arthur naval base a few years later.

After China suffered a debilitating defeat by the Eight-Nation Alliance in the Boxer Rebellion of 1900, Russia boldly pushed even farther eastward, expanding its territory in Manchuria. Russia's border moved closer and closer to Japan, backing the island nation into a geopolitical corner. Even the great European powers were concerned about the Czar's aggressive expansion in the Far East. Japan believed that its only recourse was to take preemptive action.

These political cartoons were published at the start of the war, reflecting the opposing Russian and Japanese views of the situation.

A doorway for a Great Power—entrance to one of Asia's best harbors. Port Arthur, Manchuria. Copyright 1904 by Underwood & Underwood.

THE DRAGON STRIKES

In late 1903, Archie and Boilerplate were touring Japan with an international scientific delegation that included Russian scientist, teacher, and author Konstantin Tsiolkovsky, the father of astronautics and rocket dynamics. The two men hit it off, and Tsiolkovsky invited Archie to visit his home in Kaluga, Russia. They planned to stop over in Port Arthur until the spring thaw, then head north to Vladivostok and ride the new Trans-Siberian Railway.

Unfortunately, they happened to be in Port Arthur on February 8, 1904. In the wee hours that Sunday morning, fast-moving Japanese torpedo boats launched a surprise attack on the Russian naval squadron anchored there, sinking three ships. Japan later blockaded the harbor and commenced a land-based siege of Port Arthur.

"Though I admit to some sympathy toward the Japanese point of view, I am greatly disappointed in their tactics. As for the Russians, they are ill prepared and perennially disorganized, and only two days past they lost their best Admiral—Mokorov—and his entire flagship to a floating mine. Disaster seems to seek them out.

"I know not how long Boilerplate and I will remain hemmed in here, nor when this missive may reach you, but you can be sure that we shall keep safe and return to Japan as soon as circumstance permits."

—Archibald Campion, letter to Lily Campion (April 15, 1904)

Boilerplate in Port Arthur, Manchuria, just before the Japanese Army's siege of the city. February 1904.

The Japanese predawn surprise torpedo attack on the Czar's fleet at Port Arthur.

Underwood & Underwood, Publishers.
New York, London, Toronto-Canada, Ottawa-Kansas,

CLASH OF THE TITANS

The Russo-Japanese War involved nearly a million troops and caused hundreds of thousands of casualties. Russia's vaunted Baltic Fleet made a grueling seven-month journey to the Pacific, in an attempt to relieve Port Arthur. Upon arrival, the fleet was decimated in a single afternoon by the Imperial Japanese Navy during the Battle of Tsushima Strait.

Throughout the siege of Port Arthur, Boilerplate provided crucial yet neutral support by making supply runs through territory too dangerous for humans. Despite being well provisioned, the exhausted Russians surrendered Port Arthur in January 1905. Archie was immediately granted safe passage to Tokyo. He and Boilerplate never made it to Kaluga.

LESSONS UNLEARNED

During Japan's land siege of Port Arthur, Gen. Nogi Maresuke's *human wave* tactics resulted in the massacre of 56,000 Japanese soldiers. They suffered heavy losses and failed to break through Russian lines—thus proving that an infantry charge, no matter how massive, could not take an entrenched position defended with mechanized weaponry. Sadly, this lesson was not learned by the European powers. A decade later, during World War I, generals repeatedly gave orders for similar suicidal tactics, much to the dismay of Archie Campion.

⬆ Japanese howitzers bombard Port Arthur, August 1904.

⬅ Japan's newly built rail system meant that it could join in Western traditions such as this touching goodbye between soldier and sweetheart in 1905. The war with Russia placed Japan front and center on the world stage. The smaller Asian nation managed to adopt the technologies of the West while retaining many aspects of its own ancient culture.

Japanese lie dead at the bottom of Russian defensive trenches at Port Arthur, mown down by the Russians' newfangled machine guns.

One of the greatest sea battles in history took place between Japan and Russia at Tsushima Strait in 1905. Not since the Battle of Trafalgar, a century earlier, had the world seen a nautical conflict of such scale and political impact.

Boilerplate accompanies Prince Mikeladzy, chief of gendarmes, on his rounds of the Russian defensive positions, just below one of the forts at Port Arthur.

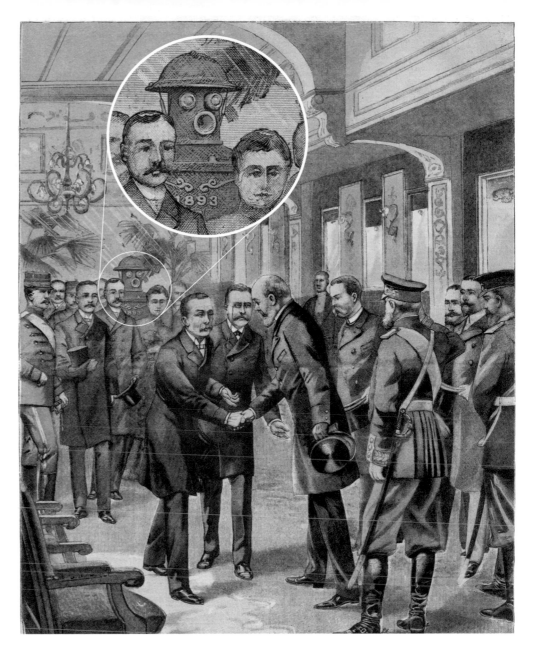

← Boilerplate finds itself the center of attention from Russian soldiers. Archie Campion chose to remain neutral in the Russo-Japanese War, resisting both sides' attempts to requisition Boilerplate for military duty. He was among hundreds of Western noncombatants, including journalists and foreign military observers, in Manchuria during the war.

→ President Teddy Roosevelt introduces the Japanese and Russian representatives at the close of the Russo-Japanese War, 1905. In the background are Archie and Lily Campion, with Boilerplate.

After Archie's first visit to Japan in 1899, he became one of Teddy's most trusted advisers on Japanese matters. Japan was generally thought of in the U.S. as a simple country of artisans, but Archie intrigued the military-minded Teddy with descriptions of Japan's ancient martial traditions. When Archie immobilized Teddy with a simple jujitsu move, Teddy developed an avid interest in the martial art and the country.

Jigoro Kano, the founder of judo, taught Archie the jujitsu move that so impressed Teddy. Jujitsu and judo involve breaking an opponent's balance and using his own strength against him. Archie convinced Teddy that Japan's foreign policy was analogous to judo, as demonstrated by the small island nation's defeat of imperial Russia in the Russo-Japanese War.

THE TREATY OF PORTSMOUTH

By that summer, Russia was losing to the Japanese, as well as being wracked by revolutionary uprisings at home. Japan had also suffered an enormous financial and human cost. U.S. President Teddy Roosevelt worked behind the scenes to persuade both combatants to conduct peace negotiations, which culminated in the Treaty of Portsmouth being signed on September 5, 1905. Roosevelt was awarded the first Nobel Peace Prize for his role in ending the first major war of the twentieth century.

Although Archie disapproved of Japan's sneak attack on Russian ships early in the war, he was also disappointed that Japan, the decisive victor, was denied compensation for war costs. The Japanese and Russian citizenries, their expectations inflated by their respective governments, both felt shortchanged by the Treaty of Portsmouth.

"It is a good thing that the war ended as it did, without the Japanese getting an enormous indemnity and with them still facing Russia in East Asia. I have a most friendly feeling for Japan; but it would be a bad thing for her and all mankind if the hopes of her admirers such as Archibald Campion had been fulfilled; for evidently the Japanese people have been in great danger of having their heads turned."

—President Theodore Roosevelt, letter to Henry Cabot Lodge (1905)

Curious locals watch as Boilerplate helps a Tokyo merchant.

This apocryphal scene depicts Boilerplate paying respects to Fukuzawa Yukichi, one of the founders of modern Japan. Fukuzawa was born into a samurai family, but he became an influential author, teacher, translator, and political theorist. He helped shape Japan's transition from feudal to modern during the remarkable Meiji era.

金属人間尊重を捧ぐ

BIRTH OF A GREAT POWER

Japan's triumph over Russia in a full-scale, high-tech war shocked Western nations. Only fifty years earlier, Japan had been a feudal country in self-imposed isolation, complete with lords in castles and samurai knights. Its most sophisticated art was sword-making. After being strong-armed into allowing visits from U.S. naval squadrons, Japanese rulers realized their nation had to change in order to survive.

Taking a massive lurch forward in just a few decades, the Japanese embraced new technology and new modes of communication, transportation, industry, and warfare. The Russo-Japanese War was the first war to rely on telegraphs and telephones, machine guns, barbed wire, mine fields, advanced torpedoes, and armored battleships. The scale of the casualties, and the war's potential to spread to Europe, alarmed observers.

"The civilized world was staggered . . . Are civilization and progress to receive a setback from which there will be no escape for centuries? Is the peace of the world threatened and are the powers of Europe, and perhaps our own country, on the verge of a great struggle?"

—Publisher's Preface, *Exciting Experiences in the Japanese-Russian War* (Henry Neil, 1904)

Defeating a major world power put Japan squarely on the global stage and helped make it confident enough to eventually confront the United States. In 1941, when the Empire once again felt threatened, it launched another preemptive strike using the same tactics that had proven so effective at Port Arthur. In the early hours of a Sunday morning, the Imperial Japanese Navy sent swift torpedo attack craft against a fleet of important battleships, anchored in a port named . . . *Pearl Harbor.*

Lily and Archie Campion pose with Boilerplate and their Japanese guide outside a shop in a merchant district of Nagasaki, 1905. As a significant port city, Nagasaki was known for international trade. The signage in English and Russian reflects the dominant economic powers of the day.

PRINCESS ALICE
1884–1980

Through Archie's friendship with Teddy Roosevelt, Lily Campion developed a lifelong bond with the remarkable Alice Roosevelt, Teddy's daughter. Both women were beautiful, smart, outspoken, and—despite the difference in their ages—just a tad on the wild side. The newspapers loved them.

Young Alice, T. R.'s only child by his first wife, was notorious for shocking behavior, such as wearing makeup, driving a car, walking around without a chaperone, and smoking in public. She charmed international high society nonetheless, and her 1906 wedding to Congressman Nicholas Longworth was the biggest gala in White House history.

Occasionally, Alice's star power proved politically useful. In 1905 Lily, Alice, and Longworth toured Asia as part of a U.S. goodwill delegation, led by Secretary of War (and future President) William Howard Taft. Archie and Boilerplate, recently released from the lengthy siege of nearby Port Arthur, met up with them in Japan. Alice and Lily distracted the press, while Taft held secret negotiations with Japanese Prime Minister Katsura that paved the way for the Treaty of Portsmouth to end the Russo-Japanese War.

Among Lily and Alice's mutual friends was Broadway actress Ethel Barrymore, sister to John and Lionel Barrymore and great-aunt to Drew Barrymore. Whenever Lily, Alice, and Ethel were in the same city at the same time, the trio hosted salon discussions together, attended the very best balls, and waltzed with the very best men, from actors to royalty. Ethel famously turned down a marriage proposal from Winston Churchill.

Alice Roosevelt was a fixture in Washington, D.C. society until 1980, eventually earning the nickname the other Washington Monument. She lived to the ripe old age of ninety-six.

Alice on T. R.:

"My father always wanted to be the bride at every wedding, the corpse at every funeral, and the baby at every christening."

T. R. on Alice:

"I can be President of the United States, or I can control Alice. I cannot possibly do both."

Ethel Barrymore, the most celebrated actress of her era, was close friends with Alice Roosevelt and Lily Campion.

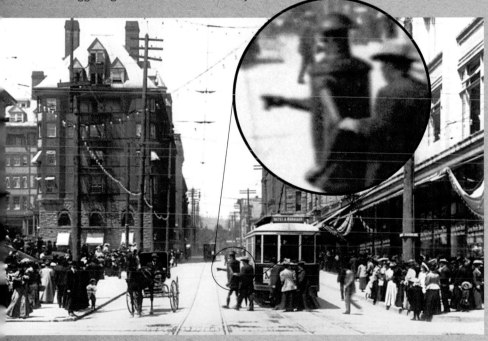

↑ Boilerplate and Archie Campion, followed by Lily Campion and Alice Roosevelt, crossing Morrison Street at Fifth Avenue in Portland, Oregon, 1905. They stopped there on the way home from Asia, staying at the stately Portland Hotel, the red brick building in this photo. The hotel was demolished in 1951 and replaced with a parking lot.

← Three of the most famous women of the day and the men in their lives. In the red dress is Lily Campion. Clockwise from her are Ethel Barrymore, Lionel Barrymore, Archie Campion, Teddy Roosevelt, and Alice Roosevelt.

Alice Roosevelt, regarded as America's princess, meets Japanese princesses in Tokyo. Archie Campion and Boilerplate are behind Alice.

VIVA LA REVOLUCIÓN!

Eighteen years after they first met in Cuba during the Spanish-American War, Boilerplate served under Black Jack Pershing in Mexico. Pershing, who was a general by then, recruited the mechanical man in 1916 for a mission to pursue the famous Mexican rebel leader Pancho Villa.

Francisco "Pancho" Villa, revolutionary Mexican general and erstwhile governor of Chihuahua, raided a New Mexico border town in 1916. When the American Army went after Villa, it brought along Boilerplate.

THE PUNITIVE EXPEDITION

The Mexican Revolution that began in 1910 dissolved into a civil war between previously united factions led by Villa, Venustiano Carranza, and Emiliano Zapata. Much to Villa's annoyance, Carranza was installed as president of Mexico, with U.S. backing. On March 9, 1916, Villa led a deadly raid on Columbus, New Mexico. His goal was political, not material, gain: He hoped to provoke a U.S. military intervention in Mexico that would rally peasant support behind his own faction, the Villistas.

It worked. President Woodrow Wilson sent 12,000 U.S. Army troops into Mexico to capture Villa and destroy his forces. Commanded by Gen. Pershing, this punitive expedition marked the first time airplanes and motorized ground vehicles were used in an American military action. Pershing requisitioned the latest technology available: the newly formed 1st Aero Squadron, Vickers-Maxim machine guns, and *Roosevelt's mule*, aka Boilerplate.

→ General John Pershing and his aide with Boilerplate at the start of the punitive expedition against Pancho Villa in 1916. Pershing met Boilerplate more often than anyone except Teddy Roosevelt. Black Jack first saw the robot in action in Cuba during the Spanish-American War. Pershing, then a lieutenant, commanded the black cavalry units that reached the top of San Juan Hill before Roosevelt's Rough Riders.

Having also witnessed the robot's effectiveness in reconnaissance missions over rough terrain in the Philippine-American War, Pershing requisitioned Boilerplate in 1916 for his punitive expedition against Pancho Villa. Two years later, he got Boilerplate involved in European operations during WWI, which led to the automaton's disappearance.

⬇ The staging area for the departure of Pershing's punitive expedition, near Columbus, New Mexico.

Boilerplate and a wireless communications wagon outside Casas Grandes near the U.S. border. Other high-tech items were also used on this expedition, such as aeroplanes and machine guns.

FIRST FLIGHT OF THE AIR FORCE

The punitive expedition of 1916 marked the first time the U.S. used airplanes in a military operation. In this photo, Boilerplate helps a Curtiss JN-4 Jenny biplane taxi for takeoff. The plane is part of the newly formed 1st Aero Squadron, predecessor of the Army Air Force, which in turn was the predecessor of the USAF.

Jennies, although popular, were nowhere near as effective as the biplanes then being flown in Europe during WWI. The JN-4 was unarmed, underpowered, and unstable—it couldn't fly over the mountainous terrain Pancho Villa was hiding out in. Instead of reconnaissance and bombing missions, Pershing had no choice but to use his airpower in a mere courier role. Capt. Benjamin Foulois, seen here in the cockpit, went public with his frustration. A *New York World* article complained that the airmen were *"risking lives ten times a day, but are not given equipment needed."*

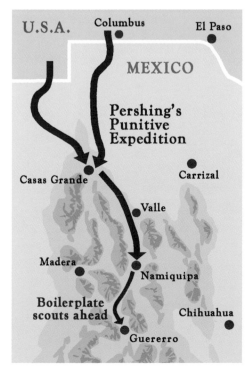

U.S.A. Columbus   El Paso

MEXICO

Pershing's Punitive Expedition

Casas Grande   Carrizal

Valle

Madera   Namiquipa

Boilerplate scouts ahead   Chihuahua

Guererro

"THEIR BULLETS WERE LIKE GNATS"

Boilerplate was attached to the all-black 10th Cavalry (of San Juan Heights fame), under Col. William Brown, and assigned to conduct long-range reconnaissance. Flying columns of the 10th pushed south into the Santa María Valley of Mexico, in pursuit of Villa.

Pershing hoped that the robot, which could traverse rough terrain quickly and tirelessly, would be able to gather intelligence on Villa. On March 19, 1916, the mechanical soldier was scouting ahead of the Buffalo Soldiers along the campaign route, nearly eighty miles south of Brown's position. There, in the secluded town of Namiquipa, Boilerplate came face to face with Pancho Villa.

"Suddenly there was a great commotion. Someone cried out that an American soldier had been captured and was being led to the hotel where Villa was headquartered. I went outside to see for myself, and a stranger sight I have never witnessed. This American was not a man at all—nor did it seem possible this being could ever be taken prisoner, for he was formed entirely of metal and stood a head taller than even the tallest man. A large blanket was fastened about his shoulders, so that from a distance he appeared as an ordinary peasant.

"I later learned that our lookouts north of town had fired on him as he approached, but their bullets were like gnats to this giant. Rather than retaliate, the metal figure asked to be taken to their leader. Thus he marched down the main street flanked by the lookouts, accumulating spectators as they proceeded."
—U.S. Army interview with Modesto Nevares, captured Villista (July 1916)

The unusual meeting lasted for two hours. It is unclear what, if anything, Boilerplate actually said to Villa. Afterward the Villistas left Namiquipa, having learned from one of their scouts that two hundred Carrancista soldiers were closing in on them. However, once Villa realized that his troops

The 10th Cavalry in Mexico's Santa María Valley

outnumbered his opponent's, the Villistas turned around and defeated the Carrancistas in a fierce firefight. The following day, Villa and his men marched out of town again, with a hundred more horses and new weapons.

THE ACCIDENTAL SAVIOR

Boilerplate remained in Namiquipa until the 10th Cavalry arrived two days later. The robot informed Col. Brown that Villa planned to attack Guerrero, a Carrancista stronghold nearly a hundred miles to the south. Unfortunately, the route to Guerrero lay across a maze of canyons and a mountain range that topped 11,200 feet. And Villa had a two-day head start.

The weary 10th set out after Villa. At the same time, Col. George Dodd and the 7th Cavalry were also bearing down on Guerrero. Boilerplate, again scouting ahead, reached the town first. On March 28, when Villa attacked Guerrero, the mechanical man found itself in the midst of a pitched battle between Villistas and Carrancistas.

During one of Villa's charges, an enemy gunner had a clear shot and fired a dozen rounds at him. But Boilerplate moved into the line of fire, just in time to block the bullets. Only one bullet hit Villa, in the leg. Historians still debate

Boilerplate runs alongside Pancho Villa as his cavalry known as *Los Dorados, the golden ones,* ride toward an engagement with Carrancista forces. Before the day was out, the robot would save the Mexican rebel leader's life.

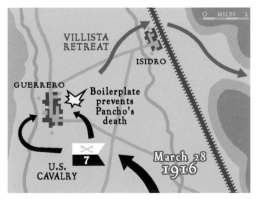

whether the mechanical man intentionally prevented Gen. Villa's death.

The Villistas won control of Guerrero, but Villa left town on a stretcher that evening. He couldn't risk being captured by the Americans. The next day, U.S. Cavalry forces took the town and killed nearly fifty Villistas. Villa hid out in the mountains, recuperating and reorganizing.

Archie and Boilerplate went back to the States in June 1916, after American troops clashed with federal Carrancista forces in the Battle of Carrizal. Boilerplate wasn't involved in the battle, which almost caused a war between the U.S. and Mexico.

General Pershing never caught Villa, and the U.S. expedition left Mexico in February 1917—just two months before the United States entered World War I. Mexican President Carranza was ousted from power in 1920; his successor granted Villa a pardon. Three years later, the retired revolutionary Pancho Villa was shot to death in a quarrel over money.

To date, the Villistas are one of only two groups of foreign fighters to attack the United States on its own soil and get away with it.

BUFFALO SOLDIERS

Throughout Boilerplate's time in the racially segregated American military, the robot repeatedly served with the heroic black combat regiments known as the *Buffalo Soldiers*. Boilerplate saw action with them in Cuba, the Philippines, China, Mexico, and France. They were among the most highly decorated veterans of these conflicts, receiving twenty Medals of Honor—more than any other unit.

Buffalo Soldiers got their nickname from Native Americans during the Indian Wars of the nineteeenth century. Some sources say it's because their hair and complexion reminded Native Americans of the American bison. Others say it's because the buffalo symbolizes bravery.

Long posted on the frontier, the Buffalo Soldiers were unaccustomed to blatant racism when they were sent east in preparation for the Spanish-American War. The *Tampa Morning Tribune* wrote: "*The colored infantrymen stationed in Tampa . . . insist on being treated the way white men are treated.*"

Boilerplate was with the Buffalo Soldiers at Las Guasimas and San Juan in Cuba, when they rescued the Rough Riders from being pinned down by heavy Spanish fire. In the acclaimed but disorganized charge up Kettle Hill, Col. Roosevelt's men were intermingled with troops from the all-black 9th and 10th cavalry. It was the standard of the 10th that first flew atop the hill, planted by Sgt. George Berry.

After the Spanish-American War, Boilerplate was reunited with the 9th and 10th Cavalry during the Philippine-American War, the punitive expedition against Pancho Villa, and the Boxer Rebellion. The paradox of black troops fighting Apaches, Mexicans, Cubans, Spaniards, Fillipinos, and Chinese, in the service of white men's ambition, was not lost on the Buffalo Soldiers.

Boilerplate last served with Buffalo Soldiers during the Meuse-Argonne campaign in WWI, fighting alongside the 370th Infantry, a National Guard regiment from the robot's hometown of Chicago. The *Black Devils*, as their French allies called them, were the only combat unit entirely commanded by black officers.

These soldiers were particularly fond of Boilerplate, as a U.S. soldier treated with disrespect by its own army. Despite being repeatedly underestimated, both the robot and the Buffalo Soldiers proved themselves to be among the finest soldiers in military history.

⬅ **Previous page:** General Pancho Villa and his staff pose with Boilerplate near the town of Guerrero, Mexico, on March 27, 1916. Villa enjoyed publicity and novelty; the robot brought him both.

This famous photo has prompted some historians to speculate that Boilerplate warned Villa about the approaching U.S. forces. Others insist that the robot was incapable of the independent volition required for such an act.

Army Medal of Honor circa 1900

CHAPTER 5

THE WAR TO END ALL WARS

—— *or* ——

BOILERPLATE'S FINAL BATTLE

By the time Boilerplate and Archie returned to the U.S. from Mexico in June 1916, Europe had been engulfed in World War I for two years. Back then it was known as the *Great War* or, with unwitting irony, the *War to End All Wars*.

London, January 1917. Archie and his Mechanical Marvel sell war bonds at the base of Nelson's Column in Trafalgar Square. The square commemorates Admiral Horatio Nelson's victory over Napoleon in the Battle of Trafalgar in 1805. Nelson, commanding the English fleet from aboard the flagship HMS *Victory*, destroyed the French fleet off the coast of Trafalgar, Spain, dashing Napoleon's plans to invade England.

METAL MAN OF ARABIA

The United States hadn't yet declared war. Archie got stonewalled when he tried to convince the U.S. War Department to requisition even a single squad of mechanical soldiers. His offers to absorb most of the cost fell on deaf ears. Even Maj. Gen. John "Black Jack" Pershing, who would ultimately help win the war, couldn't prevail on the government to adopt Archie's proposal.

Dismayed, Archie decided to try his luck in London, where he had contacts in the British military. Winston Churchill, the Minister of Munitions in England, had met Boilerplate while serving under Lord Horatio Kitchener in the African Sudan before the turn of the century. Churchill declared that he knew of "*the perfect assignment for an indefatigable mechanical soldier*" with desert railroad experience.

And that's how the robot met Lawrence of Arabia.

Winston Churchill was, in a way, the English equivalent of Teddy Roosevelt: author, soldier, and *bon vivant*, best known for leading his country during World War II.

DOMINO EFFECT

World War I began in 1914 as a conflict between Austria-Hungary and Serbia. Within weeks, the Central Powers (Germany, Austria-Hungary, and the Ottoman Empire) were at war with the Triple Entente (Russia, France, and Great Britain), triggered by their obligations under a precariously complex set of international agreements and alliances. The war was widely—and wrongly—expected to be brief, even as it expanded to affect millions of people in dozens of countries all over the planet.

The centuries-old Ottoman Empire, based in Turkey, was crumbling at the edges yet still a potent foe. After losing its last remaining territory in Europe during the Balkan Wars of 1912–1913, it clung tightly to control of the Middle East. Most of today's national borders there, such as those delineating Iraq, Iran, Israel, and Saudi Arabia, didn't yet exist.

The Middle East became a major theater of operations for the Brits during WWI. At first the goal of their Egyptian Expeditionary Force (EEF) was to protect Great Britain's control of Egypt, the Suez Canal, and the Anglo-Persian oil pipeline in what's now Iraq. But the British later shifted to a more aggressive steategy, aiming to

The shot heard 'round the world. A Serbian nationalist assassinated the visiting Archduke Franz Ferdinand, heir to the Austro-Hungarian throne, in Sarajevo on June 28, 1914. The political motive was local, but the result was global: It set off World War I.

World War I was waged on multiple fronts in at least four different theaters—European, Middle Eastern, African, and Pacific—and at sea in the Atlantic and Mediterranean. The European theater included the Western Front, Eastern Front, Balkan states, and Italian Front.

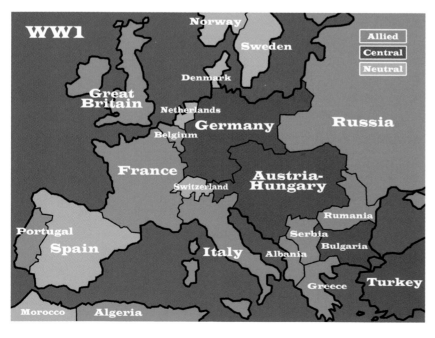

Boilerplate and Archie set out to find Lawrence of Arabia, March 1917.

knock the Turks out of the war and divvy up the Ottoman territories with France.

Churchill sent Archie and Boilerplate to Egypt in late March 1917. When they departed from London, British forces had just captured Baghdad on the eastern side of the Arabian Peninsula but failed to take Gaza in the northwest.

"I am bound once more for desert terrain, against my better judgment. Experience has taught me to prefer ice to sand. Bitter cold causes but a negligible effect on my metal man, whereas air-borne grit and scarcity of water are together potentially ruinous. As for myself, I would far rather meet my end in Arctic slumber than suffer blistering dehydration.

"Then there is the question of purpose. If we succeed in hastening Britain's defeat of the Turk in Arabia, will this fulfill my mechanical soldier's purpose by preventing the deaths of men? Is that purpose, in itself, a worthy one if the consequence is to augment the military puissance of belligerent nations? Answers may come another day. In the present instance, I must believe that our cause is just."

—Archibald Campion, letter to Edward Fullerton (March 28, 1917)

"ON THE ENDLESS SANDS"

From Egypt, Archie and his automaton made their way to the Hejaz region on the western coast of Arabia, bordering the Red Sea south of Gaza. They were met by a Bedouin, who guided them to a remote desert camp and introduced them to an amazing sight: an Englishman decked out in Arab robes. This was Capt. T. E. Lawrence of the British Army, he who would later be mythologized as Lawrence of Arabia. Boilerplate had just joined the Arab Revolt against Ottoman rule.

"Because Lawrence so closely studies the Bedu way of living, even adopting it to some extent, he has won the tribesmen's respect and succeeded in shaping them into an effective (albeit erratic) martial force. This young captain may be the most insightful, original man I shall ever chance to meet. And he cuts a dashing figure out here on the endless sands, so much at ease in his native raiment. You would doubtless find him quite appealing."

—Archibald Campion, letter to Lily Campion (April 12, 1917)

Lawrence of Arabia and Boilerplate in 1917, just before crossing the Nefud Desert to capture Aqaba.

T. E. Lawrence was a British liaison officer who convinced rival Arab factions to cooperate in attacks supporting Allied military objectives during WWI. Lawrence's dashing exploits were sensationalized by reporter Lowell Thomas, and ultimately given grand Hollywood treatment as an award-winning cinema epic directed by David Lean.

DEMOLITION DUTY

Throughout the spring, Boilerplate assisted Lawrence and his band of Bedouins in a series of crippling strikes against the Hejaz

Railway. It was the region's only railroad, a thin lifeline through harsh terrain—and the Turks' only means of moving troops and supplies from their southern base in Medina to the northern war zone, where they were battling the British in Palestine. Lawrence's goal was not to destroy the railroad, which the Brits planned to use after winning the war, but rather to temporarily disable it.

Occasionally Lawrence's target was an isolated outpost along the railway, or a train carrying armed troops. He soon learned to put Boilerplate in the lead of such attacks. The robot simultaneously intimidated jittery Turkish guards and deflected their bullets, lending extra protection and enthusiasm to the Arabs charging along behind it.

Boilerplate detonates explosives to derail a Turkish troop train. Lawrence, standing next to the robot, prepares to fire a signal flare to coordinate an assault on the train by his Arab guerrillas.

"Captain Lawrence is gaining repute for what some consider an entirely new methodology of warfare, but which is more accurately viewed as the ingenious application of an ancient methodology: employing small, swift raiding parties to disrupt the enemy's lines of supply.

"Being woefully outnumbered, lacking in modern military training and ordnance, this tiny band cannot hope to defeat the Turk in a battle of any significant scale. Yet Lawrence turns this to their advantage by utilizing their fighting style in the service of Britain's—and their own Sherif Hussein's—larger strategies. Thus my automaton, having once laid a railroad across Africa, is now demolishing another in Arabia."

—Archibald Campion, letter to Frank Reade Jr. (April 14, 1917)

Typical station along the Hejaz Railway.

THE SUN'S ANVIL

In June 1917, Boilerplate and Archie embarked on a much more ambitious mission with Lawrence. The charismatic, diplomatic young Englishman assembled a patchwork army of Bedouins from different tribes and convinced them to cooperate toward a common goal: driving the Turks out of Aqaba, an important seaport at the northern tip of the Red Sea.

The British Navy couldn't secure Aqaba by sea, because the Turks had heavy artillery in the hills surrounding the town. The guns were in a fixed position, pointed out at the Red Sea. The only route to attack them by land lay across the scorching, deadly Nefud Desert—and no one could be crazy enough to try crossing the Nefud. So Lawrence's Arab army did exactly that.

Boilerplate carried enough extra water for a dozen men during the dangerous crossing, while Archie protected the robot from sand damage. Lawrence's forces survived their grueling trek and took Aqaba by complete surprise from the north in early July. They easily captured the Turkish garrisons one by one.

"All the Turks we met were most happy to surrender, holding up their arms and crying 'Muslim, Muslim' as soon as they saw us. They expressed . . . no intention of adding a Moslem enemy to the powers already against them. . . . With the prisoners (now about 600 in number) and our Tin Man, we marched into Akaba on the morning of July 6. The astonishment of a German N.C.O. (well-boring at Khadra) when the Sherif's force appeared was comic. He knew neither Arabic nor Turkish, and had not been aware of the Arab revolt or its mechanical mascot."

—Captain T.E. Lawrence, "The Occupation of Akaba," *Arab Bulletin* No. 59 (August 12, 1917)

Boilerplate joins Lawrence of Arabia and Bedouin tribesmen in guerrilla raids on the Hejaz Railway. Boilerplate was well suited for demolition work, but sand was a constant danger to the robot's joints. The raids hindered the enemy by delaying the movement of men and supplies, and by forcing the Turks to divert resources to protect and repair the railway.

Boilerplate acts as honor guard for Gen. Allenby's entrance into Jerusalem.

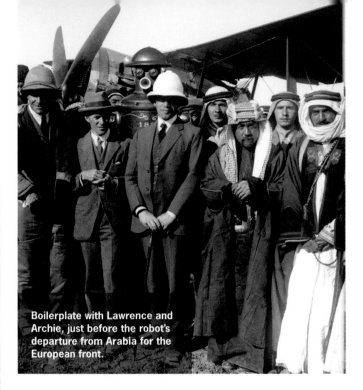

Boilerplate with Lawrence and Archie, just before the robot's departure from Arabia for the European front.

AFTER AQABA

In the meantime, England had dispatched Gen. Edmund Allenby to assume command of the EEF in the Palestine campaign. Allenby sent orders to Aqaba, transferring Boilerplate to the 60th (2/2nd London) Division of the EEF under Gen. Philip Chetwode.

For the next few months, Boilerplate fought shoulder-to-shoulder with British soldiers in Palestine as they captured Beersheba, Gaza, and finally—on December 9, 1917—Jerusalem. They took more than 12,000 Turkish prisoners. It was the first time in 500 years that any conquering forces had set foot in Jerusalem.

"The London troops and their mechanical yeoman had displayed great endurance in difficult conditions. The London troops especially, after a night march in heavy rain to reach their positions of deployment, had made an advance of three to four miles in difficult hills in the face of stubborn opposition.

"I entered the city officially at noon, December eleventh, with a few of my staff, the commanders of the French and Italian detachments, the heads of the political missions, and the Military Attaches of France, Italy, and America . . . The population received me well. Campion's automaton is regarded with considerable awe and is, one suspects, a strong deterrent to any would-be insurrectionists."

—General Edmund Allenby, Report on the Fall of Jerusalem (December 1917)

THE WESTERN FRONT

On a map of Europe, the Western Front is a squiggly line cutting southeast across Belgium and France, from the North Sea to Switzerland. On the ground, it was millions of men living and dying in miserable, muddy trenches and underground chambers called *dugouts*.

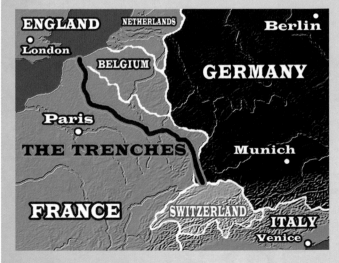

BACK TO THE FRONT

Archie and Boilerplate parted ways with Allenby after Jerusalem. The United States had joined the war while they were riding with Lawrence, and newly promoted Gen. John Pershing was commanding the American Expeditionary Force in Europe. Pershing sent word to Archie that his mechanical soldier was needed on the Western Front.

In Europe, where the Allies were suffering heavy losses, news of Allenby's victories in Palestine provided a much-needed morale boost. Allenby remained in the Middle East and went on to win his greatest victory, the Battle of Megiddo, in September 1918. The Turks signed an armistice on October 30, 1918, and the Ottoman Empire was no more.

As planned, Ottoman territory was divvied up among European powers after the war, ostensibly for short-term guidance and protection as neophyte nation-states. National borders were drawn (and later redrawn) by the European powers, who largely ignored age-old sectarian, tribal, and ethnic differences among the region's nomadic tribes. Great Britain took control of Iraq and Palestine, including areas that are now Israel and Jordan. The British soon appointed Emir Faisal, a leader in the Arab Revolt, as King of Iraq. France was given a mandate to oversee Syria and Lebanon. The last French troops left Syria in April 1946.

"DOCUMENTS ARE LIARS"

"Remember that the manner is greater than the matter, so far as modern history is concerned. One of the ominous signs of the time is that the public can no longer read history. The historian . . . learns to attach insensate importance to documents. The documents are liars. No man ever yet tried to write down the entire truth of any action in which he has been engaged. All narrative is parti pris . . . We know too much, and use too little knowledge."

—T. E. Lawrence, letter to Lord Lionel Curtis (December 22, 1927)

After the Allies blocked the initial German advance in late 1914, both sides dug elaborate trench systems, stretching for hundreds of miles. The trenches, meant to shelter troops from machine gun and artillery fire, also practically immobilized the vast opposing armies. For four bloody years, the attacking German forces tried to push toward Paris and conquer France, while Allied troops struggled to beat them back. Neither side gained more than a dozen miles until 1918.

"Actually the Hun seems to be the least of our problems. In addition to the snails coming out of the dugout walls when it rains, we have trench rats visiting us nightly. They can shred leather shoes like lettuce. And then we have another interesting little critter: the 'Cootie.' Cooties [lice] are always with us. If only we were all made of metal like our Tin Man, the critters would leave us be, and we'd never be cold or hungry again. I dare say we wouldn't need trenches at all."

—Pvt. Arnold Hahn, letter to Mary Hahn (May 1918)

German soldiers who died defending their line. Millions of men on each side of the Western Front endured hellish conditions in the trenches, more dying from disease than in combat. A minor wound could easily become infected and, without antibiotics, be fatal.

THE YANKS ARE COMING!

The American military, despite its success during the Spanish-American War, was still understaffed, underequipped, and barely trained when the United States declared war on Germany in 1917. In short, it was not up to the job.

So when Gen. John Pershing took charge of the American Expeditionary Force, he took on the herculean task of forming, training, and transporting a massive army from scratch. Not only did he do it—using a motley assortment of borrowed and commandeered civilian ships to help ferry men across the Atlantic—he also held firm on two pivotal points:

★ Pershing directed that all American soldiers must be trained in offensive open warfare, rather than defensive trench warfare. The stalemate along the Western Front had become a war of attrition, and Pershing figured the best way to break the deadlock was to go on the attack.

★ He insisted on sending U.S. troops into battle as complete units under American command. This frustrated other Allied military leaders, who wanted to use U.S. soldiers as individual replacements, scattered throughout the various national armies. But Pershing stood fast, and President Wilson backed him up.

As a result, American troops didn't see combat until autumn 1917, and then only in small numbers. At first they were attached to veteran French, Australian, or British outfits for combat training. Gradually, as the Yanks proved themselves in battle and their ranks swelled with fresh arrivals, Pershing's plans were realized. By mid-1918, the U.S. was sending 10,000 soldiers to France every day.

On August 10, 1918, the American First Army—the nation's first official field army—was formed. Boilerplate was inducted into the First Army as a master specialist, in recognition of the metal man's honorable and wide-ranging military service. It was the only rank the mechanical soldier would ever hold, and no other soldier in the U.S. Army would hold that rank again until 1955.

The entry of a whole new army on the Allied side was the last straw for the flagging Central Powers. One by one, they dropped out of the war. The fighting finally ended on the eleventh hour of November 11, 1918, when the armistice with Germany took effect.

That night, millions of men clambered out of dank, dark trenches to warm themselves around bonfires. They no longer had to fear that the firelight would reveal their positions to the enemy. For the first time in four years, the Western Front shone bright under the stars.

"Permanent peace, however; peace based upon social justice, will never prevail until national industrial despotism has been supplanted by international industrial democracy. The end of profit and plunder among nations will also mean the end of war and the dawning of the era of 'Peace on Earth and Good Will among Men.'"

—Eugene V. Debs, "The Prospect for Peace" (1916)

A repurposed freighter serves as a transport vessel for U.S. forces and Boilerplate, crossing the English Channel in early 1918. The robot had just returned from serving with Lawrence of Arabia and Gen. Allenby in the Middle East, and was on its way to join Gen. Pershing in France.

Before entering World War I, the isolationist U.S. had a standing army of only 126,000 men, and therefore had no need for a fleet of troop transports. When America joined the war, it needed to get two million new soldiers across the Atlantic, but didn't have nearly enough military vessels. The feat was accomplished using cargo ships, about half of which were provided by the British.

"The character of ships which we had gathered signified our lack of a merchant marine force. Above the gunwales of their grey sides was a crowded mass of khaki uniforms, amidst which the sharp-eyed observer could spy a gleam of copper: a mechanical soldier within the ranks, prepared as the rest to face the Hun."

—Frederick Palmer, *My Second Year of the War* (1917)

General John Pershing, commanding the American First Army, addresses Allied generals in Paris: *"The variety in instruments of war created by man reflects his martial character. It was an American who devised a metal soldier to relieve men of war's most dangerous and arduous duties. Whereas the Hun has built a cannon that shells cathedrals from many miles away."*

YOU'RE IN THE ARMY NOW

During the final year of World War I, Boilerplate and Archie Campion were at last called to arms by the U.S. military. The rapidly mobilized American Expeditionary Force (AEF) had finally joined the fighting in France, providing welcome relief to the Allied armies that had been fending off German attacks for three long years.

When Boilerplate and Archie returned to Europe from Palestine in March 1918,

U.S. forces were just starting to arrive in large numbers. And the Germans had just launched the *Spring Offensive*, pushing back the battered Allied lines forty miles in only eight days.

Southeast of Paris, in Chaumont, Archie and his mechanical soldier found the man who had summoned them to France: Boilerplate's old acquaintance Gen. John Pershing, commander of the AEF.

SPIKING THE PARIS GUN

General Pershing immediately dispatched Boilerplate on a special mission to protect Paris, which was being shelled by German artillery from the astounding distance of seventy-five miles away. The typical range of artillery fire in 1918 was only twenty-five to thirty miles.

The Germans' *Paris Gun* fired 250-pound shells that soared to a stratospheric

Boilerplate's first mission in the European theater was spiking this massive German gun.

height of twenty-five miles—higher than any other manmade object flew until the first V-2 rockets were launched in 1942. Its aim wasn't precise, but its psychological effect was devastating. Paris had been breached by enemy fire.

Although the Allies later discovered that at least three giant guns were bombarding Paris, initially they thought there was only one. Boilerplate set out to sabotage it after French pilots spotted its location. The robot snuck behind enemy lines to Coucy Forest near Laon, where it spiked the enormous cannon. Next time the Germans tried to fire it, the gun exploded, killing five of its seventeen-man crew.

THE TIDE TURNS

After Boilerplate successfully completed the Paris Gun mission and returned to Pershing's headquarters, Archie spent two weeks training a small group of military engineers in the simpler aspects of the robot's operation and maintenance. Pershing planned to send his new robotic recruit to a series of strategic points on the front lines. Archie was to stay with the General Headquarters staff so that he'd be easy to find when the metal man needed repairs.

From June through August 1918, Boilerplate fought in decisive battles that helped reinvigorate the Allies' fighting spirit and change the course of the war.

"I was surprised to find myself feeling akin to a mother sending her only son off to wage war. Capable and durable though Boilerplate may be, I confess to a nearly constant fear for its safety. This war is a particularly brutal one by all accounts, dominated by the impersonal, implacable march of technology. I wonder if my mechanical man is truly a solution, or merely another novel weapon as you have suggested. I wonder too if you were similarly fearful when Hugh—if you will forgive me for raising the spectre of his memory—departed for Corea."

—Archibald Campion, letter to Lily Campion (June 6, 1918)

➡ Boilerplate with an American *doughboy*. U.S. soldiers acquired the nickname in the pre-Civil War southwest, based on the dust-covered desert infantrymen and the adobe structures they were quartered in. The term *doughboy* was in common parlance during World War I, but died out after the U.S. government's cruel treatment of WWI vets during the Bonus March of 1932. By WWII, *G.I.* and *Yank* had become the popular terms for American infantrymen.

⬇ Boilerplate's superhuman strength was invaluable in battlefield tasks such as quickly positioning heavy equipment or, in this case, clearing debris from rail lines.

▶ Because this was the first time tanks were used in war, there were as yet no antitank weapons. Desperate attacks such as the one seen here were the only way to immobilize these strange metal behemoths.

⬇ A French messenger dog delivers important orders through a town decimated by artillery and gas attacks.

WAR OF THE FUTURE

World War I was a global conflict on a scale never before seen, involving new, high-tech vehicles and weapons such as aeroplanes, tanks, machine guns, and poisonous gas. At times it had a nightmarish, science-fiction quality, as seen in these stark images.

⬆ In only a decade, airplanes evolved from sluggish, barely controllable motorized kites to nimble instruments of death. A WWI military pilot's life expectancy was about one week. Nevertheless, aviation was still such a novel and romantic undertaking that there was no shortage of new recruits.

➡ Old meets new: a German lancer and his steed wear gas masks to protect against chemical weapons. In previous wars, jousting-style cavalry charges were a standard tactic. In WWI, they proved futile against mechanized weaponry.

BATTLE OF BELLEAU WOOD
JUNE 3-26

American troops won the day in this fierce engagement, a joint counterattack with the French 10th Colonial Division. Boilerplate helped the 4th Brigade of the U.S. Marines halt the German advance at Belleau Wood, alarmingly close to Paris. As the Marines marched toward the battlefield, fleeing civilians and French troops ran in the opposite direction, shouting that the war was lost.

Undeterred, the robot and the Leathernecks assaulted a solid wall of German machine guns. It took six attempts over three weeks, and cost 1,811 American lives, until at last Boilerplate and the Marines drove back the enemy. In honor of their tenacity, the French renamed the woods *Bois de la Brigade de Marine.*

"Issued December 8, 1918, in honour of the 4th American Brigade, fighting at Belleau Wood. This brigade consisted of two regiments of Marines with an experimental Machine-Soldier, and a Machine-Gun battalion from the 'Regulars' of the U.S.A.

"Thanks to the brilliant courage, vigor, dash, and tenacity of its men, who refused to be disheartened by fatigue or losses; thanks to the ingenuity of American science; thanks to the activity and energy of the officers; and thanks to the personal action of Brig. Gen. Harbord, the efforts of the brigade were crowned with success, realizing after twelve days of incessant struggle an important advance over the most difficult of terrain and the capture of two support points of the highest importance, Bouresches village and the fortified wood of Belleau."

—French Government Citation in Honor of 4th American Marine Brigade (December 8, 1918)

"C'MON, YOU SONS OF BITCHES! DO YOU WANT TO LIVE FOREVER?"
—Gy. Sgt. Dan Daly, 4th Marine Brigade (June 6, 1918)

Boilerplate and U.S. Marines stop the German advance in Belleau Woods, June 1918.

SECOND BATTLE OF THE MARNE
JULY 15–AUGUST 5

Germany tried to launch one last major offensive before there were enough American units in combat to tip the scales, but it was too late. Boilerplate and 85,000 U.S. troops, along with French and British forces, turned the German attack into a disastrous German defeat. It was the first in a string of Allied victories that ultimately ended the war.

"On this occasion a single regiment of the 3rd Division wrote one of the most brilliant pages in our military annals. It prevented the crossing at certain points on its front, while on either flank the Germans who had gained a footing pressed forward. Our men, firing in three sections, met the German attacks with counterattacks at critical points and succeeded in throwing two German divisions into complete confusion, capturing 600 prisoners. Of those, at least 200 surrendered to Campion's automaton."

—Gen. John Pershing, Report on the Second Battle of the Marne (August 1918)

Boilerplate goes over the top in a classic example of an infantry assault in trench warfare. Although such a direct attack on enemy trenches was an oft-used tactic, it was rarely successful. A more effective strategy was to first covertly cut as much barbed wire as possible, then attack at night.

BATTLE OF AMIENS
AUGUST 8–11

Boilerplate was attached to the 33rd Division, the sole American unit involved in this clash. The Battle of Amiens launched the Allies' decisive *Hundred Days Offensive*. Allied forces advanced more than seven miles on the first day alone, later described by German Gen. Erich Ludendorff as "*the black day of the German Army.*"

At Amiens the Allies employed *peaceful penetration* tactics: Tanks, machine guns, and Boilerplate provided a creeping barrage to protect the advancing infantry. Modern tactics such as this helped break the trench warfare deadlock. They were a marked improvement over many earlier battles, in which wave after wave of unprotected infantry were mowed down by gunfire during poorly planned assaults on fortified trenches.

◀ Boilerplate and Allied infantry advance across *no man's land*, the deadly area between opposing trench lines. No man's land was a strip of cratered mud, punctuated by rows of barbed wire, littered with rubble and human carnage from repeated assaults. It formed a nearly continuous trough of desolation, 100 to 300 yards wide, all the way across France from Belgium to Switzerland.

⬇ Boilerplate rides atop a tank as a column of the high-tech, all-terrain fighting vehicles advances into no man's land. Tanks were among the new inventions that drastically changed the nature of warfare in the early twentieth century, rendering trench warfare obsolete. Initially dubbed *landships*, during their development they were called *water carriers*, then *tanks*, for secrecy. Even the workers assembling them in factories at first thought they were making a new type of water transport.

1918-B "Campion's Marvel" at the Place de Halles, St. Mihiel.

END GAME

In September 1918, Gen. Pershing put the newly formed American First Army—seven divisions, more than half a million men, and one robot—into action in a campaign to break through German lines at St. Mihiel. It was the largest offensive operation ever undertaken by U.S. armed forces.

As it turned out, the Germans had already started withdrawing from St. Mihiel, so they were defeated with relative ease. Archie Campion's mechanical soldier was in the vanguard of the American operation, which netted 16,000 prisoners and secured an important railway communication line for the Allies.

At the same time, Pershing had to prepare for the even larger Meuse-Argonne campaign, which was part of a concerted Allied offensive all along the Western Front. In this final series of battles, he commanded more than a million American and French soldiers, including those who had fought at St. Mihiel. In preparation for the attack, 600,000 Americans troops covertly moved into the Meuse River valley while 200,000 French troops moved out.

⬆ Boilerplate stands amidst the ruins of St. Mihiel, after the town was captured by the Allies in September 1918. Because combat zones were entrenched during most of WWI, collateral damage to towns such as this was limited—especially in comparison to U.S. bombers' massive destruction of European cities during World War II.

THE LOST BATTALION

On October 2, 1918, Gen. Pershing ordered the U.S. 77th Division to *"take the Argonne Forest by frontal assault if necessary—no matter what our casualties are."*

A mixed battalion of about 600 men commanded by Maj. Charles Whittlesey advanced into the woods, encountering light resistance. They reached a defensible position and dug in for the night. But in the dense forest and incessant rain, they didn't notice that they had outpaced the rest of the 77th—or that German units had encircled them from behind, cutting off any hope of relief.

By October 5, the Lost Battalion had run out of food and water. The next day, Pershing sent Boilerplate, laden with all the supplies it could carry, behind German lines to find Whittlesey's men. The metal soldier delivered the supplies and returned to report on the battalion's exact location. Then, on October 7, the robot took part in the assault that broke through German lines to relieve the 194 surviving members of the Lost Battalion.

During that assault, Boilerplate vanished without a trace.

In the confusion of battle, the robot's absence wasn't noticed until that evening. Despite an exhaustive search, not even a

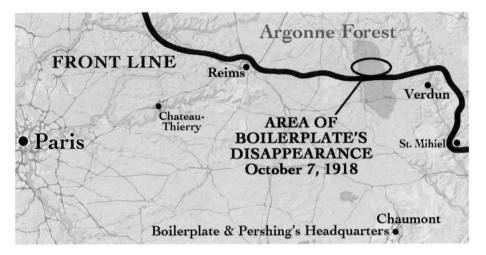

fragment of the mechanical soldier was ever found. There is some speculation, but no hard evidence, that it was captured and studied by the Germans. Boilerplate's true fate remains a mystery.

A shell explodes directly in front of the American line in the Argonne Forest. This is the last known photograph of Boilerplate.

Germany, with broken sword in hand, bows down in surrender to the Allied nations, ending the Great War. Many Germans viewed the Treaty of Versailles as a betrayal, because it forced their nation to accept unduly harsh surrender terms. This wave of resentment helped enable the rise of the Nazi party and WWII.

PANZERMANN

In the years after World War I, many rumors circulated about Boilerplate's fate. Rather than being destroyed by an artillery shell, could the mechanical man have been captured by the Germans?

Some adventurous historians have speculated that the rapid advancement in certain areas of German technology before World War II was based on secret studies of Boilerplate. Others point to the fact that some of

An artist's speculative rendering of Panzermann.

Germany's cutting-edge technology came from American corporations—for example, an IBM subsidiary reportedly sold technology to the Nazis that enabled them to efficiently identify and transport Jews, including a numerical identification system that the Nazis employed by tattooing ID numbers on people's arms.

German scientists may indeed have had an opportunity to study Boilerplate's design. During World War II, the Nazis inventoried an incomplete copy of Boilerplate's schematics when they occupied Paris in 1940. They found the documents in the archives of the Conservatoire des Arts et Métiers, part of a collection donated in the 1930s by Professor Tryphon Tournesol, a friend of Archie Campion's. The Nazis transferred the documents to Berlin, where they were apparently captured by the Soviets in 1945. When the Soviet Union collapsed a half-century later, many of its classified records were released. The files containing Boilerplate's schematics, like the robot itself, had gone missing.

Just as Boilerplate sightings occasionally occurred in the U.S. after the robot disappeared, there were reports of an automaton fitting Boilerplate's description in Germany during the 1920s and 1930s. But the existence of the elusive metal figure, nicknamed *Panzermann*, was never proven.

ONE OF A KIND

Archie Campion was devastated by the loss of his robot. As a child, he had weathered the deaths of his parents and brother-in-law by single-mindedly devoting himself to inventing an indestructible man. Without realizing it, he created a family member that could never die—and now was gone forever. He was just as deeply affected by the long-delayed realization that he would never be able to prevent the deaths of men in the conflicts of nations.

European commanders, despite having seen the high cost and futility of Japanese infantry attacks against entrenched Russian guns during the Russo-Japanese War, employed the same outdated tactics in World War I. The Allies routinely lost up to 7,000 men every day, and many more during big battles. Archie grew increasingly outraged by watching the same mistakes repeated in different wars.

"How is it that educated men may so thoroughly fail to heed the lessons of history? Perhaps it is for the best that Boilerplate is lost, for I desire no further involvement with military matters. I vow there shall never be another such prototype."

"And how is it that an educated man such as myself may so thoroughly misunderstand the military and political minds? I now realize that nations would use armies of mechanical men to wage even deadlier and more destructive wars. I am infuriated by my own slow-wittedness."

—Archibald Campion, letter to Edward Fullerton (October 16, 1918)

To prevent any future military use of his invention, Archie abandoned his robotics research, destroying most of his notes. So far, no one has been able create a functioning duplicate of Professor Campion's Mechanical Marvel.

THE FORGOTTEN MAN

Returning soldiers had a hard time adjusting to civilian life after WWI. There was no G.I. Bill or Veterans Administration, and posttraumatic stress disorder wouldn't be recognized for another half century. When the Great Depression hit in 1929, most vets found themselves homeless with little recourse. They marched on Washington, D.C., in 1932, demanding the veteran bonuses they'd been promised—and the United States government called out the Army against them. On July 28, Gen. MacArthur and Maj. Patton led U.S. troops that attacked U.S. veterans on the streets of Washington, killing several and wounding hundreds.

"A man who is good enough to shed his blood for his country is good enough to be given a square deal afterwards. More than that no man is entitled to, and less than that no man shall have."
—President Theodore Roosevelt, speech to veterans, Springfield, Illinois (July 4, 1903)

"Remember my forgotten man,
You put a rifle in his hand.
You sent him far away,
You shouted, 'Hip, hooray!'
But look at him today!"
—Al Dubin and Harry Warren,
 "Remember My
 Forgotten Man" (1933)

"Bring Them Home"

Archie and Lily Campion in the 1920s.

EPILOGUE: LIFE AFTER BOILERPLATE

Archie Campion's robot was part of a lost generation of advanced technology—along with electric cars and Edward Fullerton's hydrogen fuel cells—that had to be discovered all over again decades later. These technologies could have been commercially viable if they had been developed at the time. Instead they went dormant, largely due to corporate disinterest or opposition, until the late twentieth century.

As nimble-minded as ever, Archie continued to create the occasional patentable invention for fun and profit. He studied theoretical physics, eventually teaching physics as well as ethics at the University of Chicago. He was well known in scientific circles, and was a regular invitee at the international Solvay Conference on Physics. Archie maintained lifelong contact with his old friends Frank Reade Jr., Edward Fullerton, and Nikola Tesla.

Archie had also learned, the hard way, that technology alone can't solve human problems. He joined his sister, Lily, in social

FORWARD INTO LIGHT

Lily spent decades fighting for women's right to vote, often with Archie's help. She co-founded the International Council of Women in the 1880s, and, in the 1890s, she joined forces with Carrie Chapman Catt to help women win full enfranchisement in populist western states such as Colorado and Idaho. In the early 1900s, Lily helped forge an alliance between wealthy suffragists and the labor movement on the East Coast.

She wrote articles, gave speeches, and marched along with thousands of others, including Boilerplate, in suffrage parades. She was thrilled when women gained voting rights in New Zealand (1893), Australia (1902), and Finland (1906), but dismayed that her own nation had not yet seen the light.

When Lily, Ida Wells, and Boilerplate took part in a famous 1913 demonstration calling for universal suffrage in Washington, D.C., Lily was shocked that the organizers asked black suffragists to march at the rear of the parade. Wells refused, instead rejoining the Illinois delegation while the parade was in progress. Lily proudly marched next to her.

As this cartoon points out, even after women won the right to vote in western states, eastern states refused to follow suit.

In 1916, Lily was instrumental in getting Montana suffragist Jeanette Rankin elected as the first woman in Congress. Rankin soon proposed a constitutional amendment to enfranchise women. At long last, in August 1920, the Nineteenth Amendment to the U.S. Constitution was ratified by three-quarters of the country's state legislatures, and American women won the right to vote.

"Forward out of darkness, leave behind the night, forward out of error, forward into light!"
—Motto of the National Woman's Party

⬆ At the 1913 voting rights march, left to right: reporter Nellie Bly, philanthropist Lily Campion, suffragists Lucy Burns and Alice Paul, astronomer Henrietta Swan Leavitt, and mathematician Virginia Ragsdale.

The word *suffragette* originally referred specifically to members of the Women's Social and Political Union, a radical faction of the women's suffrage movement in the United Kingdom. The more general term *suffragist* was preferred by other activists in the U.K. and U.S. Both words derive from *suffrage*, which means the right to vote.

⬇ Official program book for the women's suffrage demonstration in Washington, D.C., March 1913.

→ The tomb of Archie and Lily Campion, in Graceland Cemetery on the north side of Chicago.

← Lily Campion on horseback, accompanied by Boilerplate, during a massive suffrage march on Washington, D.C., 1913.

↑ Famed cartoonist Winsor McCay charts the notable participants in the 1913 suffrage demonstration, including one Mrs. Lily Campion.

→ A reprint edition of Lily's most famous novel.

activism, supporting a variety of foundations and even influencing policymaking in Washington, D.C. Through their friendships with Teddy, Alice, and Franklin Roosevelt, the Campions helped shape both the Square Deal and the New Deal—economic programs that raised the nation's standard of living, expanded public health protections, and built up public infrastructure such as highways, bridges, airports, utilities, parks, and libraries. In 1936, the Campion siblings were honored with the first Abigail Adams Award for their commitment to social justice.

Despite having endured a harrowing siege in Peking and other dangers abroad, Lily never lost her taste for travel. When she eventually grew too frail to go jaunting around the world, she brought the world to others by teaching international history and writing globetrotting romantic adventures with strong heroines. Lily's most popular novel, *Lady Ace*, was the story of an English aviatrix who disguises herself as a man in order to join the British Royal Flying Corps during WWI.

Lily survived both Archie and World War II, living a full century. She died peacefully at her friend Alice Roosevelt's house in 1952.

Late in his life, Archie helped preserve a piece of Boilerplate's and Chicago's past: the former Palace of Fine Arts, the last remnant of the World's Columbian Exposition. After the fair, the building briefly housed the Field Museum of Natural History until 1920, then sat vacant. With financial and political backing from Archie and fellow philanthropist Julius Rosenwald, the building was extensively renovated starting in 1929. It reopened as the Rosenwald Industrial Museum—later known as the Museum of Science and Industry—in 1933, just in time for Chicago's A Century of Progress world's fair.

Twenty years after his globe-spanning exploits with Boilerplate ended, Archibald Campion died where he was born: in Chicago, Illinois, on October 30, 1938. He was, alas, upstaged even in death. The next day's headlines reported a panic about interplanetary invasion, courtesy of young actor Orson Welles and his radio broadcast of *The War of the Worlds*.

Orson Welles.

CHAPTER 6

POPULAR DEPICTIONS OF BOILERPLATE

⟿ *or* ⟿

THE ROBOT, REMEMBERED

From native Hawaiian songs to video games, Boilerplate has been mythologized and memorialized in all kinds of ways for more than a century.

This cigar advertisement, which appeared the year Boilerplate was unveiled, is a veritable who's who for 1893.

This was the first ad Boilerplate appeared in, and the only one Archie ever appeared in. The juxtaposition is incongruous, considering that Archie hated tobacco. After an initial flurry of ads featuring Boilerplate, Archie decided that he didn't want his robot to be a huckster, and became more selective about publicity engagements.

The metal man's first wave of notoriety peaked while it was on active military duty during the Spanish-American War in 1898. Stephen Crane reported on the automaton in one dispatch, Richard Harding Davis covered it in two others, and Teddy Roosevelt wrote about the *mechanical mule* in his book *The Rough Riders*.

After Boilerplate vanished in 1918, its fame soon faded. But every few decades, a spark of interest flares anew in the public imagination, and the robot is rediscovered by pop culture. Archie's mechanical man has inspired Boilerplate dime novels, comics, movies, toys, costumes, art, jewelry, ephemera—even occasional sightings. Presented herein is a sampling of the many artifacts and anecdotes devoted to Professor Campion's Mechanical Marvel.

Left to right in facing image: Professor Archibald Campion, Campion's Mechanical Marvel, John Drew Jr. (actor related to the Barrymores), Thomas Palmer (head of the World's Columbian Exposition Commission), General John Schofield (commanding general of the U.S. Army), "Buffalo Bill" Cody (renowned Wild West showman), Alexander Herrmann (world's most famous magician, before Houdini), President Grover Cleveland, and Chauncey Depew (railroad magnate, later a U.S. senator and adviser to President Theodore Roosevelt).

THRILLING RESCUE OF THE CHILD, BY THE METAL MAN. AND HEADLONG FALL OF THE VILLAIN INTO THE DEPTHS OF CHILKOOT CAÑON.

JACK AND THE ROBOT

Boilerplate encountered writer Jack London on several occasions, such as while London was fortune-hunting in the Yukon and, later, reporting on the Russo-Japanese War.

At the same time that London found success as an author, magazines became the dominant popular medium, thanks to new printing technology that made them cheap and plentiful. His early novel *Marvel of the Klondike,* a string of fictionalized tales about Boilerplate in the Yukon, grafted a few of Boilerplate's real adventures onto a fictional narrative about Archie Campion prospecting for gold and striking it rich. London omitted the fact that Archie's real-life millions came from patents, not precious metals.

The stories were serialized in magazines in 1898, adapted as a collection of stage vignettes in 1899, and later turned into a movie serial. Unfortunately, no footage from or advertisements for the cinematic version are known to exist.

⬆ Poster for the 1899 theatrical adaptation of Jack London's Boilerplate serial.

➡ No tall tale of frontier life is complete without someone wrestling a bear. Boilerplate never actually did this, but it's easy to see why the imagery was irresistible to Jack London.

⬅ Writer Jack London, who penned an early series of Boilerplate tales, is best known for enduring classics such as *Call of the Wild.* His existential adventures, colloquial language, and championing of the underdog blazed a trail for later authors such as Jack Kerouac.

DIME-NOVEL DAYS

Boilerplate Weekly Magazine, which ran for 104 issues between 1902 and 1904, is doubtless the source of some confusion about the robot's true history. Like his friend Frank Reade Jr., Archie Campion and his inventions were the subject of wild science-fiction tales, only a few of which were even loosely based on actual events.

The stories were written by the same author: a young Cuban American named Luis Senarens, credited in print as *Noname*. His Frank Reade yarns were so popular that Senarens was the publisher's first choice to pen the Boilerplate dime novels.

PULP FICTION

Dime novels were inexpensive, mass-market books published from the mid-1800s to roughly 1900, usually featuring sensational stories and vivid cover illustrations. It was common practice to use fictionalized versions of real people as dime-novel heroes. Buffalo Bill, Wyatt Earp, and Davy Crockett were among the early examples. Because the books were aimed at young, working-class readers, they often featured made-up "junior" versions of celebrities, such as the popular Tom Edison Jr.

Boilerplate Weekly adventures typically involved the fictional Archie Campion Jr., Boilerplate, and a fantastic invention such as a helicopter airship or an armored, all-terrain horseless carriage. The fictional Archie Jr. and his robot crisscrossed the globe, encountering even stranger lands, people, and creatures than the real-life duo ever met. They meted out justice, battled high-tech villains and exotic tribes, and occasionally unearthed fabled treasures. The series, which debuted on November 1, 1902, was a hit.

Senarens was steeped in the prevalent imperialist mindset of the late nineteenth-century United States, and his writing reflected his beliefs. Some of the attitudes in his stories would be considered outrageously

Clambering over the deck of the Dart were a number of fur-clad forms. At first the explorers thought them human beings; but a closer glance showed that they were huge white bears.

racist and inflammatory today, but wouldn't have raised an eyebrow back then. Despite being a Cuban immigrant, Senarens was a product of his times.

Archie, however, grew increasingly uncomfortable with how his fictitious counterpart was being portrayed in print. One 1904 story titled "Adventure in the Outback -or- Campion, Jr.'s Triumph Down Under," in which Boilerplate participated in an unprovoked raid on an aboriginal village in Australia, was the last straw. Archie refused to renew his license agreement with the publisher, and that was the end of *Boilerplate Weekly Magazine.*

"To my eventual chagrin, at the outset I brushed aside pangs of trepidation regarding the publishing arrangement with Tousey. Of course I understood that he cares not a whit

for scientific exploration or cultural advancement—nor, in point of fact, for anything save money—and that his dreadful writers would produce lurid tales in which my mechanical man was in some fashion mischaracterized. Yet still I believed that these popular fictions could be employed to educate the general public as to the utility of an artificial soldier.

"Alas, Tousey's magazines have instead portrayed my automaton and a 'Junior' avatar of myself as acting on the most vulgar of imperialistic motivations—geographic expansion by coercion, despoiling of natural resources, even outright theft of national treasures and sacred artifacts. I am enclosing for your delight the most recent installment, which shall be the last such embarrassment."

—Archibald Campion, letter to Lily Campion (September 1904)

EADWEARD MUYBRIDGE

Eadweard Muybridge, the forefather of cinema, established his reputation as a photographer for the U.S. Army on survey parties into Alaska and the High Sierras. He was later commissioned by a racetrack owner to prove that all four of a horse's hooves left the ground during a gallop. It was a hotly debated question at the time, and no one had yet been able to answer it definitively.

In 1877, Muybridge confirmed his patron's belief by photographing a running horse with dozens of cameras placed along a track, parallel to the moving subject. A similar setup was used in Hollywood movies more than a century later, for a different effect: freezing the subject in mid-motion and rotating the viewer's perspective around the subject.

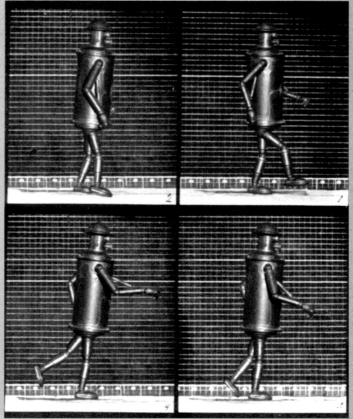

← Archie Campion prepares Boilerplate for a photo shoot by Eadweard Muybridge in 1901.

↑ Motion studies of Boilerplate, by Eadweard Muybridge.

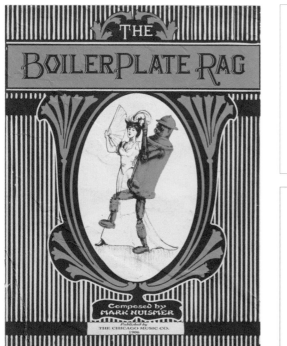

"The Boilerplate Rag" (1903) immortalized Archie Campion's robot in ragtime, the hottest style of music in the early 1900s. This early form of jazz was popularized by composer Scott Joplin, who performed on the Midway of the World's Columbian Exposition before he rose to fame. Nowadays his tune "The Entertainer" is often heard tinkling from ice cream trucks, and is known as the theme of *The Sting*. Joplin spawned hundreds of imitators who wrote songs on every imaginable subject, usually with the word *rag* in their titles.

▲ A Boilerplate movie poster, known as a *half-sheet,* from 1916. Sadly, the film itself has been lost, along with almost all films made in the silent-movie era. Because early film stock was prone to decay and extremely flammable, it was easier to dispose of potentially hazardous reels of film than to properly store and preserve them. At the time, this new medium was thought of as nothing more than pop ephemera, a flash in the pan. Few people foresaw that it would evolve into one of the greatest art forms of the 20th century.

➡ Boilerplate reviews a script with fellow actors at Essanay Studio during the 1909 shooting of *The Unexpected Guest.* This famed Chicago film studio, established long before Hollywood became the movie capital of America, was widely known in its day but has since faded into obscurity.

MECHANICAL MARVEL OF THE MOVING PICTURES

At the dawn of the twentieth century, Archie Campion and Boilerplate helped usher in a whole new medium of entertainment and communication: movies.

FRAME BY FRAME

In 1901, Boilerplate became the last subject of a series of famous motion studies by Eadweard Muybridge, the forefather of cinema. Archie commissioned the shoot after seeing Muybridge's 1899 retrospective publication, *Animals in Motion.*

This pioneering photographer used a row of still cameras, each one timed to fire less than a second after the previous one, to capture discrete moments in the movement of animal and human subjects. Archie wanted a frame-by-frame photographic record of his robot's gait in order to study the effectiveness of Boilerplate's gyroscopic stabilization.

Widespread interest in his motion studies inspired Muybridge to develop a device called the *zoopraxiscope,* which projected multiple still images in sequence, producing the illusion of movement. It was the world's first motion picture projector.

YOU OUGHTA BE IN PICTURES

Long before Hollywood became the capital of filmmaking, the fledgling industry was centered in New York and Chicago. Boilerplate did a brief stint as a movie star at Chicago's then famous Essanay Studio in 1909.

Established in 1907, Essanay specialized in Westerns and slapstick comedies. Its owners, George Spoor and Gilbert "Broncho Billy" Anderson, thought Boilerplate would be a great gimmick for their comedy *The Unexpected Guest.* They contacted Archie and offered to pay him for the robot's "acting" services. He accepted their offer on the condition that Essanay would also shoot footage of Boilerplate in motion, for his own scientific use.

Anderson and Spoor wanted to use Boilerplate in a series of Essanay films, but Archie declined to allow it. He considered pure entertainment a frivolous use for his invention, and a trivial pursuit for scientists in general.

"Moving pictures possess potential scientific value as a means of studying individual stages of continuous motion too rapid for the human eye to discern as discrete images. Yet already we

have turned this invention to the most trifling of uses. My automaton shall not play the minstrel.

"Worse, the moving picture industry, young though it be, has attained an advanced state of oligarchy. It is ruled quite roughly by the Motion Picture Patents Company, Edison's trust of studios that controls all patents relevant to equipment and film for the making of motion pictures.

"I enjoy the benefits of the patent system, as do you, and I have no argument with the concept of intellectual property in and of itself. Yet neither have I the slightest patience with bullies who wield otherwise legitimate rights as weapons to extort compliance and quash competition. That amounts to mere thuggery."

—Archibald Campion, letter to Edward Fullerton (May 13, 1909)

It didn't take long for movies to grab hold of the popular imagination. Within fifteen years after the first commercial motion picture projectors—the Edison Kinetoscope and the Lumière Cinématographe—were introduced, 10,000 nickelodeon movie theaters sprang up across the United States.

During this period, four out of every five U.S. films were made in Chicago. Essanay alone produced more than 1,400 shorts during its ten-year history, including the first Sherlock Holmes, Jesse James, and *A Christmas Carol* movies—not to mention making Boilerplate the first robot to appear in a movie. Charlie Chaplin, Ben Turpin, Wallace Beery, and Gloria Swanson are among the stars whose careers were launched at Essanay. Louella Parsons, an Essanay screenwriter, went on to become a famous Hollywood gossip columnist.

Although Boilerplate itself never acted in another movie, the robot was portrayed by costumed actors in an array of films over the years.

THE MASTER MYSTERY

Released in 1920, two years after Boilerplate went missing, *The Master Mystery* starred celebrity magician Harry Houdini as U.S. Justice Department agent Quentin Locke. The plot revolves around Locke's investigation of International Patents Incorporated for suspected violations of intellectual property rights to new inventions—such as Boilerplate. The robot is played by an actor in a particularly clunky costume.

Locke and Boilerplate foil the corporate villains' nefarious schemes, of course. Along the way, Houdini's talents as an escape artist were put to good use as Locke escapes from a straitjacket, a diver's suit, an electric chair, and being tied upside down. The serial concludes with Locke marrying a beautiful woman and discovering that he is the long-lost son of Archie Campion.

The serial was scripted by Arthur B. Reeve and Charles A. Logue, best known for *The Perils of Pauline*. *The Master Mystery* was a smash success and won Houdini a contract with Famous Players, a precursor of Paramount Pictures.

EL HOMBRE LOCOMOTORA ENCONTRE PANCHO VILLA

A late entry in the Boilerplate filmography, the 1960s low-budget Mexican film *Locomotive Man Meets Pancho Villa* was a heavily fictionalized account of the robot's 1916 encounter with Pancho Villa in Mexico. In this version of the story, Boilerplate teams up with Villa to drive U.S. forces out of Mexico, then prevents his assassination in 1923, after which Villa becomes president of Mexico.

Boilerplate models for sculpture students in a class run by American expatriate Sarah Stein—patron, critic, and confidante to Matisse, and sister-in-law to Gertrude Stein.

BUT IS IT ART?

Boilerplate seems to appeal to just about everyone, from pugilists to painters. Some writers have speculated that the robot's simplified facial features and neutral personality allow each individual to impose his or her own point of view on Boilerplate. A military commander might view the mechanical man as a weapon, for example, whereas a farmer might see it as the ultimate field hand. Personal biases also influence how different people interpret Boilerplate's face

Boilerplate, Lily, and Archie Campion at a café in the St. Germain district of Paris. Alain Loeb did this ink-and-brush sketch in 1901.

Albert Gleizes, *Automate*, 1914.

Jean-Louis Forain painted this canvas—*Les Cavaliers Rugueux*—in 1918, the year Boilerplate went MIA during World War I.

Detail from *Teddy and his Mechanical Mule* by the reclusive Nicholas Derwatt, 1948.

Piet Mondrian, *L'Homme d'Avenir*, 1912.

and stance, variously seeing the robot as sad, angry, proud, contemplative, contemptuous, or dutiful.

Visual artists tend to be fascinated by Boilerplate's anthropomorphic yet inhuman form, and impose their own symbolic interpretations on it. The robot was a particular sensation among cubist painters, who explored perception and the mechanistic nature of the modern age through geometric, multiple-perspective art styles.

"How amusing it is to see my mechanical man standing alongside one of the 'cubist' works that purport to capture its likeness! These distorted visions are of interest to me as an experiment in visual perception and representation, but I hardly consider them Art. Lily is of another mind: She thinks these cubists are brilliant beyond words and I, a Philistine. Even should she prove correct in the end, my opinion shall not waver. For what is Art that speaks not to my heart?"

—Archibald Campion, letter to Edward Fullerton (May 1914)

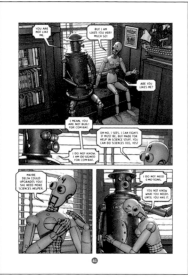

↑ "Silas," the artist of this 1909 cartoon, is actually Winsor McCay, who met Archie and Boilerplate at the 1893 World's Columbian Exposition. The exposition's White City was a direct inspiration for the artist's later comic-strip masterwork *Little Nemo in Slumberland*.

McCay was also highly influential in early animation. His 1914 short *Gertie the Dinosaur* is the first animated movie to feature a character with personality, and the first cartoon produced using the *keyframe* technique, which McCay invented. Instead of drawing each one of the thousands of frames in sequence, he first drew Gertie's key poses, then drew the frames in between those poses—a process later dubbed *in-betweening*.

↑ This graphic novel was nominated for a prestigious Eisner Award in 2006.

These pages are from the 1976 debut of Boilerplate in Mike Friedrich's groundbreaking *Star*Reach* anthology comic. It's among the first examples of what would later be called an *independent* comic book, created for the nascent *direct sales* market of comic shops, rather than for traditional newsstand distribution. Phil Seuling, father of the comic book fan convention, developed the direct sales system in the early 1980s, which paved the way for hundreds of specialty comic book stores to spring up in the U.S.

ANIMATED AUTOMATON

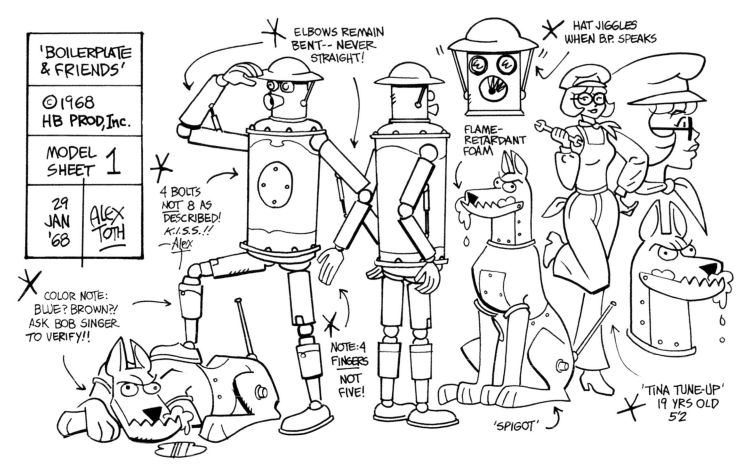

A character design sheet from *Boilerplate & Friends*, by master comic book artist Alex Toth. Toth designed many characters for Hanna-Barbera. The premise of the show was that plucky mechanic Tina repairs the long-lost Victorian robot, then the pair embarks on globetrotting adventures. The obligatory wacky mutt rounded out the cast.

➡ Frame grab from an unaired pilot for a Saturday morning animated TV series, *Boilerplate & Friends*. The series never sold, and the twenty-five-minute pilot has not been released on video.

➡ ➡ Celebrities often made inexplicable guest appearances in cartoons from this era—in this case, Zsa Zsa Gabor

COLLECTIBOTS

The Japanese company Sankei produced this walking wind-up toy, called *The Victorian Robot*, in the late 1950s.

➡ In 1903, Boilerplate's tenth anniversary, Helios Studios crafted twelve-inch brass replicas of the mechanical man. Helios was known primarily for its kinetic, sculptural timepieces and music boxes. The articulated Boilerplate figures contained a wind-up clockwork mechanism inside the chest cavity.

Ten such maquettes were made and sold for $20 each, a hefty sum back then. Only three still exist: The Musée des Arts et Metiers in Paris has one, and the other two are in private collections. Each figure's current value is estimated to be in the six-figure range.

⬆ This necklace was made in 2008 as promotional merchandise for *Sad Robots*, an album by the Canadian band Stars.

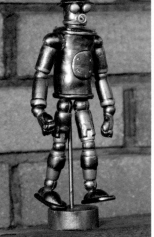

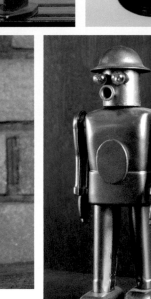

➡ A wooden push-puppet toy, manufactured circa 1970. A string inside the figure held the joints together, so that the figure would stand upright while the string was taut. Pressing a button underneath the base released the tension and made the figurine collapse. With enough practice, one could make the robot "dance" by repeatedly pressing and releasing the button.

⬆ A bootleg Boilerplate figurine made from *nonhas*, Chinese plastic building blocks, circa 2001.

⬅ Marketed under the name *Robot Soldier*, this tin wind-up robot is unmistakably Boilerplate. It was manufactured in the late 1960s by Japanese toymaker Yonezawa.

PROPAGANDA

⬆ French poster warning of the dangers of automation, 1962.

➡ Detail from a Soviet poster extolling the benefits of automation, 1937.

BOILERPLATE SIGHTINGS

⬆ Boilerplate attends a Halloween party, courtesy of die-hard fan Rich Powers. Although no officially licensed Boilerplate costume was ever released, homemade outfits have turned up at masquerades, comic book conventions, and science fairs.

WORLD WIDE WEB

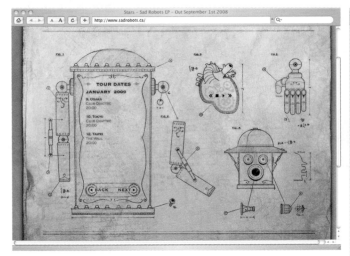

A web site promoting the Stars album *Sad Robots* includes an animated schematic of Boilerplate. The album features a photo of Boilerplate on its cover.

Boilerplate has popped up all over the World Wide Web, from tribute sites to blogs. More than a century after its creation, the robot's enigmatic charm and its inventor's naïve dream of technological salvation continue to fascinate people around the world. There's been a renewed spate of interest in Boilerplate in the early twenty-first century, as more historical material became available online.

NOW IN PRINT

Articles about Professor Campion's Mechanical Marvel are still being written. Boilerplate has appeared in international magazines such as Russia's *Paradox* and the UK's *Real Robots*.

Part of Archibald Campion's legacy is an award given out in his name. Every other year, the Campion Foundation bestows a grant on one person who has made an outstanding contribution to the field of robotics.

Boilerplate is occasionally discussed in reference works and textbooks on robotics, such as this recently published guide.

BOILERPLATE'S BRETHREN

or

MECHANICAL MEN OF HISTORY

> Boilerplate wasn't called a robot during its brief existence, because the word *robot* didn't exist yet.

The Steam Man Mark III, built by Archie Campion's friend Frank Reade Jr., on its first outing in 1879.

The term—based on the Czechoslovakian words *robota* (*compulsory labor*) and *robotník* (*serf* or *servant*)—was coined by Czech painter Josef Capek in 1920 for his brother Karl's stage play *Rossum's Universal Robots* (*R.U.R.*). It originally referred to artificial factory workers who were grown rather than built, which we would today call *clones*.

Before 1920, robots were called *automatons*. Their origins can be traced back to the ancient Greeks. The following is a brief history of Boilerplate's ancestors and contemporaries.

A scene from the 1921 play *R.U.R.*

IT'S ALL GREEK TO ME

Early automatons could perform only limited, repetitive tasks. They usually served as entertainment, or as a means of demonstrating basic scientific principles. Greek engineers produced the earliest known examples, using hydraulic and pneumatic technology that was later lost for centuries. The poet Pindar's seventh Olympic Ode, penned between 500 BC

↓ Hero of Alexandria invented the first steam-powered robots in recorded history (30–60 AD).

Al-Jazari created android servants ↑ and musicians in the twelfth century.

> "WITHOUT THE DUCK OF VAUCANSON, YOU HAVE NOTHING TO REMIND YOU OF THE GLORY OF FRANCE."
> —Voltaire

Mechanical bathroom attendant created by Al-Jazari.

and 450 BC, vividly described automatons on public display at Rhodes:

> *The animated figures stand*
> *Adorning every public street*
> *And seem to breathe in stone, or*
> *move their marble feet.*

Ancient Rhodes, a hotbed of stargazers and gearheads, was also the likely birthplace of the Antikythera mechanism (ca. 150 BC to 100 BC)—the world's first calculator or mechanical computer, designed to calculate astronomical positions. Between 30 AD and 60 AD, Hero of Alexandria combined the work of earlier engineers with his own discovery of the steam engine, and created elaborate steam-powered automatons. Among his achievements was an entirely mechanical theatrical play.

ROBOTS OF ROYALTY

Centuries later, automatons still served as diversions, but some also had practical applications. In the late twelfth century, the Arab inventor Al-Jazari created female automatons as bathroom attendants for royal clients. The attendants would stand near a basin filled with water and hand out soap. Pulling a lever flushed water from the bowl, then caused the automaton to offer towels and refill the bowl.

In 1727, at the age of eighteen, Jacques de Vaucanson built a series of automatons that acted as dinner servants, serving food and clearing tables. An influential friar of the Order of the Minims was so unsettled by the robots that he declared them profane, and had the inventor's lab in Lyon dismantled. Vaucanson went to Paris and continued his work. In 1737, he built a flutist that could play twelve separate melodies with astonishing accuracy. Two years later, he achieved notoriety by displaying a robot duck that simulated the digestive process using a revolutionary new technology: rubber tubing.

Vaucanson with his android flute player and robot duck in 1738.

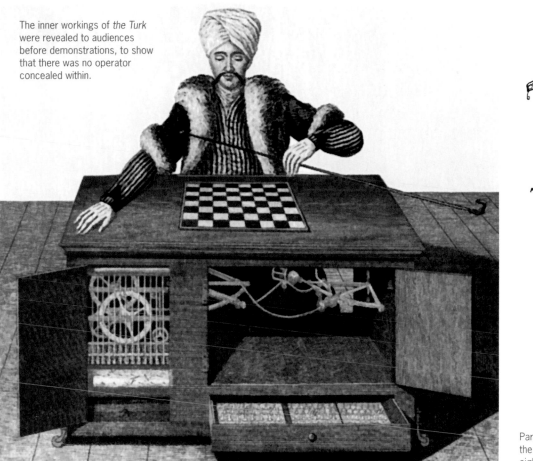

The inner workings of *the Turk* were revealed to audiences before demonstrations, to show that there was no operator concealed within.

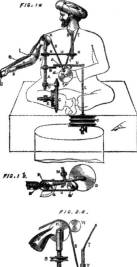

Partial diagrams of *the Turk*, the most famous robot of the eighteenth century.

CHECKMATE

The most significant eighteenth-century achievement in robotics was Wolfgang von Kempelen's chess-playing mechanical man, created on commission for Hungarian Empress Maria Theresa in 1770. The automaton was fixed in a sitting position, attached to a cabinet with a chessboard on top. The cabinet had panels that could be opened to allow detailed inspection of the inner workings, and casters so the whole contraption could be wheeled about. Because Europe was in the grip of a fad for things with a Middle Eastern flavor, the robot was dressed like a Turkish magician. It came to be known as *the Turk*.

The Turk toured the world for decades, wowing crowds and playing matches with famous figures from Benjamin Franklin to Napoleon Bonaparte. After Kempelen's death in 1804, the Turk was purchased by Johann Maelzel, an engineer and artificial limb designer, who upgraded the robot and continued to demonstrate it. When Maelzel died in 1838, the Turk was found dismantled in crates. Attempts to restore it failed because key components were missing. The Turk's remains were lost in a fire on July 5, 1854, while on display at Willson Peale's Chinese Museum in Philadelphia.

STEAM MEN

Boilerplate's first direct precursor appeared in 1868, when Zadoc P. Dederick built the Newark Steam Man. This seven-foot-tall construct was driven by a six-horsepower steam engine in its torso. It pulled an attached carriage that carried its fuel as well as passengers.

Dederick demonstrated the metal figure before thrilled spectators, including the governor of New Jersey. In some quarters, though, it raised concerns such as that put forth by the *Newark Daily Journal*: "*Will it be*

Zadoc Dederick peeks into frame in this 1868 studio portrait of the Newark Steam Man.

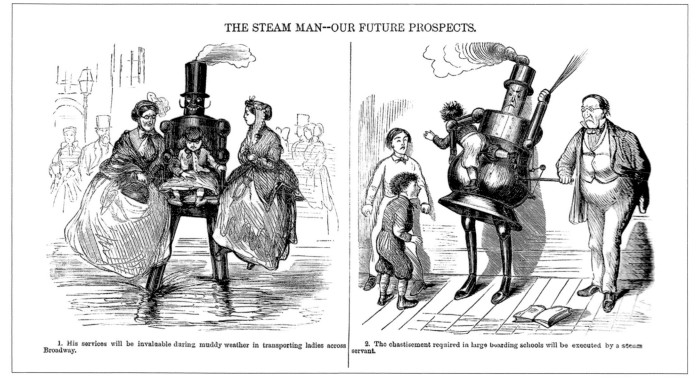

THE STEAM MAN--OUR FUTURE PROSPECTS.

1. His services will be invaluable during muddy weather in transporting ladies across Broadway.

2. The chastisement required in large boarding schools will be executed by a steam servant.

Satiric suggestions for possible uses of the Newark Steam Man. None of these whimsical vocations ever came to pass. The robot was destroyed in a fire only months after it was constructed.

possible for normal men and women to compete with steam men and women?" The Newark Steam Man was displayed at P.T. Barnum's museum in New York, but—like the Turk—was lost when a fire destroyed the museum.

Seeing the Newark Steam Man in action inspired New Jersey author Edward Sylvester Ellis to write *The Steam Man of the Prairies.* Published in 1868, it was the first book to feature what we'd now call a robot. Dederick's

work undoubtedly also influenced famed inventor Frank Reade Sr., who in 1876 built the first in a series of Steam Men.

Reade hadn't yet perfected the gyroscopic stabilization that his friend Archie Campion later employed in Boilerplate, so Reade's robots were attached to a carriage to keep them upright as they walked or ran. The carriages were also the only practical means of hauling their power sources: firewood,

The upgraded Steam Man Mark II, June 1876. Note the axe attached to the wagon, which was used to chop firewood for the robot's furnace when traveling.

coal, or enormous batteries. Reade later built a Steam Horse that ran a series of exhibition races against the Steam Men.

"*The figure is about twelve feet high from the bottom of the huge feet to the top of the plug hat which adorns the steam man's head. An enormous belly is required to accommodate the boiler and steam chest, and this corpulency agrees well with the height of the metallic steam chap. The top of the hat is a sieve, and the smoke comes out of that. The ashes from his boiler fall down into his legs and are emptied from the movable knee-pan, and without injury to the* oiled leg shafts, for they are enclosed in a tube . . . The legs are very long and very far apart, so as to give it balance. To give full working room to the very delicate machinery in his interior, the giant was made to convey a sort of knapsack upon his shoulders. The steam gauge is in the fellow's back. There's drafts and stop-offs without number. The machine holds its arms in the position taken by a man when he is drawing a carriage. It can go fifty miles in one hour, on a level road it is run at thirty or thirty-five an hour."

—Harry Enton, *Frank Reade and His Steam Man of the Plains* (1876)

◀ The Reades raced their creations at various open-air venues across the U.S. during the late 1870s and early 1880s.

⬇ Frank Reade Jr. takes the coal-powered Steam Man Mark III on its first excursion in 1879. In the back of the wagon is Pompei DuSable, whose brother Joliet helped Archie Campion construct Boilerplate. A nearby horse and a bicycle are outpaced by the new form of transport.

The Steam Horse, created shortly after the Steam Men, wound up with the same job: hauling wagons.

THE ELECTRIC HORSE

THE ELECTRIC MAN:
OF
Frank Reade, Jr.,
IN AUSTRALIA.

← Frank Reade Jr. improved on his father's steam-powered robots by creating the Electric Horse and the Electric Man, shown here during a nighttime encounter with Australian aborigines.

↓ This *Frank Reade Library* magazine recounts the final adventure of the last generation of Steam Men.

AN INVENTIVE FAMILY

It was at the first public test of the Steam Man Mark III that Reade and his children, Frank Jr. and Kate, met Luis Senarens. The fourteen-year-old Cuban immigrant had paid his own way from Brooklyn to Readestown, Pennsylvania, to witness the event. He convinced the Reade family to let him write their biographies.

New York publisher Frank Tousey, who had a publishing deal with the Reades, was skeptical about hiring such a young and untested writer. His worries proved groundless. Senarens's imaginative *Frank Reade Library* stories, although not exactly deathless prose, were so popular that Tousey later assigned him to *Boilerplate Weekly Magazine*.

Frank Jr. later surpassed his father's achievements by using a revolutionary new energy technology to power his own android: the Electric Man. Improved hydraulics and lighter-weight alloys gave the Electric Man greater strength and speed than its steam-driven predecessors. A media frenzy surrounded the robot's world tour in 1886.

The inventive Reade family went on to found Readeworks in Readestown, Pennsylvania. To this day, Readeworks is operated by their descendants and produces robotics systems for commercial as well as military use. So, in the end, Archie Campion was both right and wrong: Robots became an integral part of warfare, but they didn't eliminate the deaths of men. ★

Luis Senarens, official biographer of both the Reades and the Campions, also wrote many fictional dime-novel tales about them.

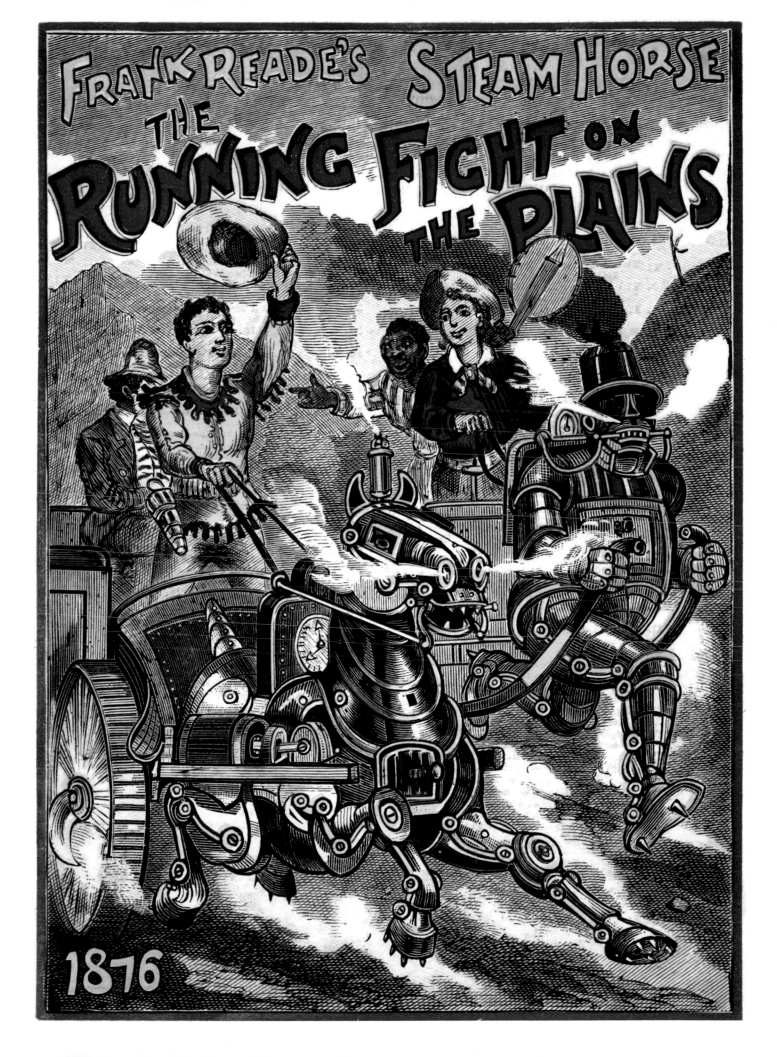

TIME LINE

Archie and Lily Campion's Prairie Avenue mansion. (1893)

February–August
Antarctica

Archie and Boilerplate trapped in ice aboard *Euterpe* for five months

September 6
Hawaii

Deposed Queen Lili'uokalani released from prison, with help from Campions

January–May
Sudan

July–December
Klondike

Gold Rush – Boilerplate gets its nickname by making publicity appearance for Oregon Boiler Works company

Archie lives with Eskimos

Jack London meets Boilerplate

A political cartoon from the Spanish-American War period, ridiculing Teddy's *"tin toy"* (1898).

May 23
Chicago

Archie Campion unveils Boilerplate at World's Columbian Exposition; tours fair on June 19

November 28
Chicago, Evanston

First car race in U.S.; Boilerplate beats winning car in exhibition race

February–December
Philippines

Philippine-American War – Boilerplate in combat, mainly as a sapper

Lily Campion travels in Asia

|1893   **|1895**   **|1897**   **|1899**

|1894   **|1896**   **|1898**   **|1900**

Spring
New York

Archie demonstrates Boilerplate in a theater appearance

May 11–July 12
Chicago

Boilerplate attached to Illinois National Guard during Pullman strike

February
Morocco

March–April
Egypt

Archie invited to demonstrate Boilerplate for Italian military in Ethiopia; they arrive too late, after Italian forces are trounced in Battle of Adwa on March 1

Archie and Boilerplate join the Geological Survey of Egypt and go on archaeological digs with Flinders Petrie and James Quibell

May–December
Sudan

Boilerplate helps build railroads for British General Horatio Kitchener, but doesn't see combat

January–March
Klondike

May–September
Cuba

Spanish-American War – Boilerplate charges up San Juan Hill with Teddy Roosevelt on July 1

July–August
China

Boxer Rebellion – Lily trapped by siege of foreign legations in Peking

Archie and Boilerplate join China Relief Expedition to rescue Lily

September–December
Archie, Lily, and Boilerplate travel to Australia with Frank Reade to ring in the new century in a new country

An advertisement by the Helios Theatre, in New York City, for Archie Campion's demonstration of Boilerplate. (1894)

Boilerplate kitted out for the Klondike. (1898)

Archie, Lily, and Boilerplate leave China for Australia aboard one of Frank Reade Jr.'s helicopter airships. (1900)

Boilerplate, Lily, and Archie play tourist in Paris. The Campions' favorite city landmark was built by Gustave Eiffel for the Exposition Universelle of 1889, and initially regarded as an eyesore by Parisians. Eiffel also designed the supporting armature for the Statue of Liberty. (1901)

Boilerplate in San Francisco, a few days after the cataclysmic earthquake and fire. The magnitude 8.0 shock was felt all along the U.S. West Coast. At least 3,000 people were killed, and hundreds of thousands left homeless, in an era when federal disaster relief was unheard of.

Gen. Frederick Funston telegraphed Archie to request Boilerplate's "immediate participation in relief efforts." Funston had seen the robot in action during the Spanish-American and Philippine-American wars. (1906)

January 1
Australia

The Commonwealth of Australia becomes official

Lily visits Aussie suffragettes

March–July
Paris

Boilerplate rides the new Metro

Archie and Lily attend shows of work by Van Gogh (posthumous) on March 17 and Picasso (first exhibit) on June 24

September
Washington, DC

Teddy Roosevelt becomes President after McKinley is assassinated; invites Boilerplate and Archie to White House

Archie sits for a portrait by renowned photographer Robert Stewart. (1903)

July 3
Gettysburg, Pennsylvania

40th anniversary of battle – Boilerplate meets Civil War veterans

September–December
Japan

Boilerplate and Archie travel with scientific delegation

January
Manchuria

Port Arthur siege ends January 2

January–July
Japan

Archie and Boilerplate meet up with Lily, Alice Roosevelt, and William Howard Taft

September
New Hampshire

Treaty of Portsmouth signed, officially ending Russo-Japanese War; mediated by T. R.

1901

1903

1905

1902

June 15
New York City

Boilerplate makes appearance at launch party for New York Central Railroad's 20th Century Limited passenger train; rides train from NYC to Chicago

November
New Mexico

Boilerplate and Archie meet Mescalero Apache tribe

1904

January
Japan

February–December
Manchuria

Russo-Japanese War – Archie and Boilerplate under siege in Port Arthur

1906

February
Washington, D.C.

The Campions attend as Alice Roosevelt marries Ohio Congressman Nicholas Longworth in a memorable White House ceremony

April–July
San Francisco

Boilerplate helps with cleanup and restoration after earthquake

November
Panama Canal

Boilerplate and Archie inspect canal construction with T. R., first U.S. president to travel outside the country while in office

Boilerplate and Little Cloud. During a trip through the American Southwest, Professor Campion spent time with the Cochise family and observed a sacred coming-of-age rite known as *Na'ii'ees*.

December 28
San Francisco

Boilerplate appears at the Cliff House to celebrate cableship *Silverton* linking telegraph cable from Sans Souci beach at Waikiki to San Francisco—first trans-Pacific telecommunications cable line

Professor Campion's Mechanical Marvel stands outside Machinery Hall at the Alaska Yukon-Pacific Exposition in Seattle. (1909)

January–February
Great White Fleet on tour

Fleet returns to Hampton Beach, Virginia, on February 22

March
New York

After his presidency, T. R. leaves for African safari; Archie and Boilerplate see him off

April–May
Chicago

Boilerplate makes movies at Essanay Motion Picture Studio

June
Seattle

Boilerplate appears at Alaska-Yukon-Pacific Exposition

September–October
Gulf Coast

Boilerplate assists with cleanup in Louisiana and Mississippi after major hurricane

December
New York

Archie and Boilerplate attend Manhattan Bridge opening ceremony

Lewis Hine was that rare artist who manages to effect meaningful social change. His photos of child laborers, some of which included Boilerplate as a sort of moral yardstick, paved the way for legislation to protect kids from deadly working conditions. (1911)

March 19
Denmark

Lily speaks at first-ever International Women's Day celebration in Copenhagen

May 23
New York

Archie and Boilerplate attend New York Public Library dedication ceremony

June–September
Archie and Boilerplate travel with photographer Lewis Hine, documenting horrors of child labor

October–November
Belgium

Archie invited to first Solvay Congress, meeting of influential physicists

March–November
Chicago

Boilerplate does trial run as cop in graft-ridden First Ward, but proves incorruptible

December
Virginia

Archie, Edward Fullerton, and Boilerplate depart with U.S. Navy's Great White Fleet on first circumnavigation of the Earth by a national naval force

1907

1909

1911

1908

1910

1912

January–December
Great White Fleet on tour

Aboard USS *Illinois*, Archie conducts top-secret fuel-cell experiment with Fullerton

April
Connecticut

Archie and Boilerplate visit Mark Twain just before his death

Halley's comet returns–Twain came in with it and went out with it

May
Nevada

Boilerplate spars with heavyweight champ Jack Johnson at his training camp near Reno

June
Germany

Archie and Boilerplate ride on first commercial flight of Zeppelin passenger airship

October
Wisconsin

Boilerplate travels with former President Teddy Roosevelt, campaigning as a Progressive

November 5
U.S. presidential election

Democrat Woodrow Wilson wins landslide victory

T. R. finishes second, ahead of Republican incumbent William Howard Taft

Socialist Party candidate Eugene V. Debs gets one million votes

Archie demonstrates Boilerplate for the Sultan of the Ottoman Empire, Mehmed V. The Sultan was installed the previous year by the Young Turks, after the forced abdication of his brother Sultan Abdul Hamid II. During World War I, Mehmed V allied with the Central Powers—and Boilerplate wound up fighting against the man who had once been his gracious host. (1910)

Boilerplate is unable to prevent Teddy Roosevelt from being shot during a campaign appearance in Milwaukee, Wisconsin. Three and a half years after leaving office, Roosevelt was running for President on the Progressive Party (aka Bull Moose Party) ticket. The bullet, fired by John Schrank, was slowed by a thick manuscript of Teddy's long speech and the steel case for his eyeglasses in his coat's breast pocket. Even with a bullet lodged in his chest, T. R. insisted on giving his speech.

A board game originally printed in a 1901 Sunday newspaper supplement. Inspired by Boilerplate's travels and Jules Verne's novel *Around the World in 80 Days*, the object of the game was for players to race each other around the globe.

February
New York

Boilerplate appears at opening of Grand Central Terminal, world's largest train station

Boilerplate-related artworks go on display in Armory Show

March
Washington, D.C.

Lily and Boilerplate march in suffragist demonstration on March 3

Ohio

Boilerplate assists with rescue and cleanup after Miami Valley floods

February–June
Washington, D.C.

Archie helps found NACA, the predecessor of NASA

Lily marches in national suffrage demonstration on May 9

August–September
Hawaii

Boilerplate helps raise sunken F-4 submarine, U.S. Navy's first sub disaster (sank on March 25)

January
London

Archie and Boilerplate help British cryptographers decipher Zimmermann telegram (German offer of U.S. territory to Mexico in return for support in attacking U.S.)

February–April
Washington, D.C.

News of Zimmermann telegram changes American opinion and helps draw United States into war

Archie tries in vain to sell President Wilson and U.S. War Department on mechanical soldiers

United States Congress formally declares war on Germany on April 6

June–December
Arabia and Palestine

Churchill invites Boilerplate to join British military campaign against Turks

Boilerplate helps Lawrence of Arabia blow up Hejaz railroad

July 6: Boilerplate and Arabian fighters led by Lawrence capture port of Aqaba from Turks

December 8–26: Boilerplate and British troops take Jerusalem from Ottoman Empire

A poster from World War I features the mechanical soldier. (1918)

1913

1915

1917

1914

1916

1918

June
Germany

Archie and Boilerplate travel on steamship *Imperator* from Hamburg to NYC, with T. R. and the Houdinis

July
World War I begins

January–February
England

Archie and Lord Horatio Kitchener attend demonstration of first tank prototypes, *Big Willie* and *Little Willie*, on February 2

March–April
Mexico

Boilerplate joins Black Jack Pershing on punitive expedition against Pancho Villa

November
Montana

With Lily's help, Jeannette Rankin becomes first woman elected to U.S. House of Representatives, before women had the right to vote in most states

January–October
France

March 23: Boilerplate goes on mission to destroy the Paris Gun, a giant German cannon that shelled Paris from 114 km (75 miles) away

June 1-26: Boilerplate fights with 4th Brigade of U.S. Marines in fierce Battle for Belleau Wood

July: Boilerplate helps defeat Germans in Second Battle of the Marne

August 8: Boilerplate fights in Battle of Amiens, on *"the black day of the German Army"*

September: Boilerplate fights in St. Mihiel campaign, largest offensive operation ever undertaken by U.S. armed forces

October: Boilerplate fights in Meuse-Argonne offensive, goes on mission to relieve Lost Battalion

October 7: During assault to rescue Lost Battalion, Boilerplate vanishes without a trace

On the promenade deck of the S.S. *Imperator*, June 20, 1914.
Left to right: Luis Senarens, Harry Houdini, Edward Fullerton, Teddy Roosevelt, Boilerplate, Archie Campion, Theodore Roosevelt Jr., Frank Reade Jr.

BOILERPLATE TODAY

Lily and Archie Campion were laid to rest in this impressive tomb at Graceland Cemetery. Established in 1860, Graceland is also the burial place of other Chicago notables such as Louis Sullivan and Daniel Burnham.

Boilerplate's first and only acting role was shot at Essanay Studio in Chicago. Once a mecca for film production, laying claim to four out of five films made in the U.S., this movie studio existed for only ten years. The structure is now a college.

Author Paul Guinan outside Archie Campion's former lab, birthplace of Boilerplate. Located on Wrightwood near Lincoln Avenue in Chicago, the building now contains upscale loft apartments.

Guinan at the *Euterpe*. The vessel that took Boilerplate to the South Pole is now docked at Chicago's Navy Pier, as part of the Maritime Museum of Chicago. Its lower decks house presentations about the ship's history, in the form of models, maps, pictures, and artifacts. Among them are photos and equipment from Campion's Antarctic expedition, with a large figurine of Boilerplate.

Archie and Lily's erstwhile home is now the Campion Foundation offices, and one of the few mansions left on the once tony Prairie Avenue.

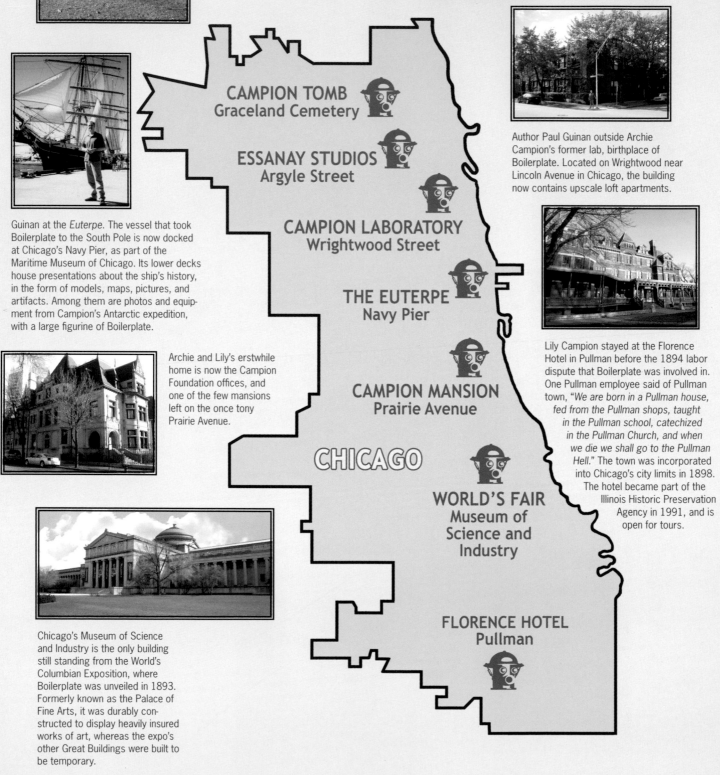

CAMPION TOMB
Graceland Cemetery

ESSANAY STUDIOS
Argyle Street

CAMPION LABORATORY
Wrightwood Street

THE EUTERPE
Navy Pier

CAMPION MANSION
Prairie Avenue

CHICAGO

WORLD'S FAIR
Museum of Science and Industry

FLORENCE HOTEL
Pullman

Lily Campion stayed at the Florence Hotel in Pullman before the 1894 labor dispute that Boilerplate was involved in. One Pullman employee said of Pullman town, "*We are born in a Pullman house, fed from the Pullman shops, taught in the Pullman school, catechized in the Pullman Church, and when we die we shall go to the Pullman Hell.*" The town was incorporated into Chicago's city limits in 1898. The hotel became part of the Illinois Historic Preservation Agency in 1991, and is open for tours.

Chicago's Museum of Science and Industry is the only building still standing from the World's Columbian Exposition, where Boilerplate was unveiled in 1893. Formerly known as the Palace of Fine Arts, it was durably constructed to display heavily insured works of art, whereas the expo's other Great Buildings were built to be temporary.

THEODORE ROOSEVELT

BOILERPLATE

⬆ Alexander Phimister Proctor sculpted this statue of Boilerplate and Teddy Roosevelt, which stands watch in a park across the street from the Oregon Historical Society in Portland, Oregon. The statue was designed with approval from the Roosevelt family and Lily Campion. Edith and Kermit Roosevelt even unearthed the uniform Teddy wore at San Juan Hill, and lent it to Proctor for reference.

Vice President Calvin Coolidge attended the groundbreaking ceremony in August 1922. Throngs of Portlanders turned out for the statue's dedication on Armistice Day, November 11. Proctor addressed the crowd, speaking about his long association with Boilerplate and Roosevelt—going way back to 1893, when he first met them at the World's Columbian Exposition in Chicago.

➡ Archie Campion with Calvin Coolidge at the groundbreaking ceremony.

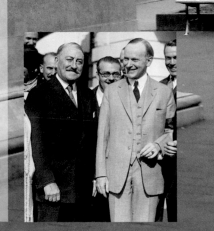

A

Addams, Jane, 26–27, 36, 64, 81
Africa, 45–47
    See also World War I, Middle Eastern theater
African-Americans, discrimination against, 26, 27, 62, 80, 104, 130
Aguinaldo, Emilio, 74, 78, 80
Alaska, 49, 50, 160
Allenby, Edmund, 114–115
Altgeld, John, 35
American Expeditionary Force (World War I), 115–128
American First Army (World War I), 19, 116, 117, 126
Amiens, Battle of (World War I), 125
Amundsen, Roald, 40
Anglo-Egyptian Nile Expeditionary Force, 45–47
Antartica expedition, 38–40, 162
Anthony, Susan B., 26
Anti-Imperialist League, 81
Antikythera mechanism (computer), 150
Aqaba campaign (World War I), 109, 112
Arab Revolt (World War I), 109–113, 115
Australia, 61, 86, 130, 136
Austria-Hungary. See Boxer Rebellion; World War I
Automate (Gleizes), 142
"automatons," 149

B

Barrymore, Ethel, 95
Baum, L. Frank, 27, 29, 31
Beato, Felice, 12
Bedouins (World War I), 109, 110–113
Belleau Wood, Battle of (World War I), 121
Berryhill, J. H., 60
Biela's Comet, 14
"Black Devils," 104
    See also "Buffalo Soldiers" (10th Cavalry)
Boilerplate
    abilities, 24, 34, 43, 75, 104, 139
    in advertisements, 132, 133
    Archie's policy on using, 36, 57, 65, 67, 82
    in art, 141–143
    co-builders of, 16, 17, 155

collectibles and toys, 28, 146
    dangers to, 108, 113
    described, 24, 28, 60, 61, 100
    design of, 16–17, 19, 28, 39, 118, 128
    disappearance of, 127–128
    fictional stories about, 134–137, 144–145
    filmography, 139–140
    introduced to world (*see* World's Columbian Exposition (1893))
    military duties, 69, 75, 76–77, 79, 85, 90, 99, 110–112, 118, 121, 122–123, 126–127
    military rank (World War I), 116
    naming of, 21, 53
    precursors to, 148–157
    publicity, on (Campion's time), 22, 28, 29, 34, 45, 51, 60, 61, 112, 122
    purpose of, 11, 28, 80, 85, 108
    time line of events, 158–161
    World Wide Web sites, on, 147
    See also specific travel locations
Boilerplate & Friends (TV series), 145
"Boilerplate Rag, The," 138
Boilerplate Weekly Magazine, 136–137, 156
Bonus March (1932), 118
Bowyer, John M., 60
Boxer Rebellion, 80, 82–87, 104
"Boxers" (Boxer Rebellion), 82, 84
Brown, William, 99–100
Bryan, William Jennings, 42
Buffalo Bill, 30, 132, 136
"Buffalo Soldiers" (10th Cavalry), 70, 99–100, 104–105
Bull Run, Battle of (1861), 9–10
Burnham, Daniel, 22, 162

C

Campion, Archie
    birth of, 10
    Chicago home, 15, 158, 162
    Chicago laboratory, 15–17, 19, 81, 162
    death of, 131, 162
    described, 15, 42, 133
    inventions, 15, 129, 140 (*see also* Boilerplate)
    parents of, 9–11
    post-Boilerplate career, 129

social activism, 36, 64–65, 129–131
Campion, Lily
    Archie's letters to, 45, 53, 89, 109, 118, 137
    and Boxer Rebellion, rescue from, 80, 82, 84–86
    Chicago home, 15, 158, 162
    death of, 131, 162
    friendship with Alice Roosevelt, 95, 131
    Lady Ace novel, 131
    marriage to McKee, 11–13
    social activism, 26, 36, 40, 64–65, 129–131
    as suffrigist, 26, 27, 130
    travels, 34, 36, 40–41, 63, 74, 94–95, 131, 159
    at World's Columbian Exposition, 24, 25, 26, 29
Campion, Robert and Jane, 9–11
Campion Foundation, 147, 162
Canada. See Klondike Gold Rush
Capek, Josef, 149
Carranza, Venustiano, 96, 101
Carrizal, Battle of (1916), 101
Catt, Carrie Chapman, 65, 86, 130
Cavaliers Rugueux, Les (Forain), 143
Chicago, 10–11, 14–15, 43
    Archie and Lily's home, 15, 158, 162
    Archie's laboratory, in, 15–17, 19, 81, 162
    Essanay Studio, 139–140, 162
    Everleigh Club, 58
    Graceland Cemetery, 162
    Hull House, 26
    Levee District, 58
    Maritime Museum, 162
    Museum of Science and Industry, 131, 162
    Pullman town, 33–36, 162
    See also World's Columbian Exposition (1893)
China. See Boxer Rebellion
Churchill, Winston, 25, 47, 95, 107, 108
Civil War, 9–10, 55
Clemens, Samuel. See Twain, Mark
Cleveland, Grover, 27, 35, 37, 81, 132
"clones," 149
Conservatoire des Arts et Métiers (Paris), 128
Coolidge, Calvin, 163
"Cooties" (lice), 115

"Coxey's Army" (1894 march on D.C.), 30, 31
Crane, Stephen, 133
Cuba. See Spanish-American War
Cubism, 143

D

Darrow, Clarence, 42
Darwinism, 42
Dawson City (Canada mining town), 48–54
Debs, Eugene, 35–37, 116
Dederick, Zadoc P., 151–153
Derwatt, Nicholas, 143
Dewey, George, 68
"dime novels," 10, 136–137, 157
"direct sales" market, 144
Dole, Sanford, 41, 61
"Dorados, Los" (Villa's cavalry), 100–101
"doughboy" (American soldier), 119
Douglass, Frederick, 26
"dugouts" (World War I), 114
Duryea, Frank, 43
DuSable, Joliet, 155

E

Edison, Thomas, 25, 140
"Edisonades," 10
Edison Kinetoscope, 25, 140
Egypt, expedition to, 44–45
Egyptian Expeditionary Force (World War I), 108–114
Eiffel, Gustave, 159
Eight-Nation Alliance, and Boxer Rebellion, 82, 84–87
Electric Man (Reade Jr. invention), 16, 156
Ellis, Edward Sylvester, 153
Eskimos, 52, 53
Essanay Studio (Chicago), 139–140, 162
Euterpe (merchant vessel), 38–40, 162
Everleigh Club (Chicago), 58

F

Fagen, David, 80
Fair Labor Standards Act, 64
Ferdinand, Archduke Franz, 108
Ferris Wheel, 27, 28
"Fight of the Century," 62–63
Filipino Army of Liberation, 79–80

Forain, Jean-Louis, 143
Ford, Henry, 27
France, 146, 159
    in World War I, 114, 115, 117–128
    See also Boxer Rebellion
Friedrich, Mike, 144
Fukuzawa Yukichi, 94
Fullerton, Edward, 36, 161
    Archie's letters to, 40, 82, 85, 108, 128, 140, 143
    co-builder of Boilerplate, 16
    fuel-cell technology, 16, 17, 19, 22, 59, 60, 129

G

Germany, 128
    in World War I, 108, 114–115, 117–128
    See also Boxer Rebellion
"Gilded Age," 30
"G.I." (U.S. infantryman), 118
Gleizes, Albert, 142
"Golden Staircase" (Klondike Gold Rush), 50, 51
Gold Rush. *See* Klondike Gold Rush
Graceland Cemetery (Chicago), 162
Gray, Elisha, 27
Grayson, William W., 75
Great Britain, 147
    Battle of Trafalgar, 92, 106
    and Boxer Rebellion (*see* Boxer Rebellion)
    World War I (European theater), 115–128
    World War I (Middle Eastern theater), 108–115
Great Chicago Fire, 11, 14, 20
Great Depression, 129
Great Financial Crisis (2008), 30
Great Panic of 1893, 30, 31, 34
"Great War." *See* World War I
"Great White Fleet," 58–62
"Great White Hope" (James J. Jeffries), 62–63
Guantánamo base (Cuba), 70

H

"half sheet" (movie poster), 139
Halley's Comet, 81
Hawaii, 40–41, 61, 70, 94
Hejaz Railway, and World War I, 110–111, 113
Helios Studios, 146
"Hermit Kingdom" (Korea), 12
Hero of Alexandria, 150

Hine, Lewis, 64, 65, 160
Hollingworth, C. K., 45
Homme d'Avenir, L' (Mondrian), 143
Houdini, Harry, 27, 140, 161
"human wave" (infantry tactics), 91
"Hundred Days Offensive" (World War I), 125

I

Illinois, USS, 17, 58, 59–60, 61
Imperator, USS, 161
"in-betweening" (cartoon technique), 144
"independent" comic books, 144
"insurgents," 80
Iraq, 108, 115
Israel, 108, 114, 115

J

Japan, 61, 80, 83, 93, 94, 95
    See also Boxer Rebellion; Russo-Japanese War
Jazari, Al- (inventor), 150
Jenny biplanes, 99
Jerusalem campaign (World War I), 114
Jigoro Kano, 93
Johnson, Jack, 62–63
Joplin, Scott, 27, 138

K

Kempelsen, Wolfgang von, 151
"keyframe" technique (cartoons), 144
"kinetoscope" (movie projector), 25, 140
Kitchener of Khartoum ("K. of K."), 45–47, 107
Klondike Gold Rush, 32, 48–54, 134, 158
"Klondikers," 50–51, 53–54
Korean War of 1871, 11, 12–13

L

Lady Ace (Lily's novel), 131
"lallapalooza" (Levee District ball), 58
"landships" (tanks), 125
Lawrence of Arabia (Capt. T. E. Lawrence), 107, 108, 109–113, 115

Lili'uokalani (Queen of Hawaii), 40–41
Locomotive Man Meets Pancho Villa (film), 140
Loeb, Alan (artist), 141
London, Jack, 30, 32, 51, 54, 134–135
"Los Dorados" (Villa's cavalry), 100–101
Lost Battalion (World War I), 127
Lumière Cinématographe, 140

M

Maine, USS, 68
Manchuria. *See* Russo-Japanese War
Manila. *See* Philippine-American War
Marconi, Guglielmo, 18
Maresuke, Nogi, 91
Marne, Second Battle of the (World War I), 122–123
Master Mystery, The (film), 140
McCay, Winsor, 131, 144
McKee, Hugh W., 11, 12–13
McKeough, Matthew, 29
McKinley, William, 68, 74, 79, 80
Meagher, William, 61
Medal of Honor, U.S., 12, 104
Megiddo, Battle of (World War I), 115
Meuse-Argonne campaign (World War I), 104, 126–127
Mexican Revolution, 96
Mexico, civil war in. *See* Villa, Pancho
Middle East, and World War I, 108–115, 160
Mondrian, Piet, 143
Museé des Arts et Metiers (Paris), 146
Museum of Science and Industry (Chicago), 131
Muybridge, Eadweard, 138, 139

N

National Child Labor Committee, 64
Native Americans, 159
Nefud Desert, in World War I, 109, 110, 112
Nevares, Modesto, 100
Newark Steam Man, 151–153
New Deal (economic program), 131

New Zealand, 130
Nobel Peace Prize, 93
"no man's land" (World War I), 124–125
"Noname" (Luis Senarens), 136–137, 156, 157, 161
"nonhas" (building blocks), 146
Northrop, Henry Davenport, 22, 34

O

Olmsted, Frederick Law, 22
"Olympic Ode" (Pindar), 149–150
Oregon, Portland Hotel in, 95
Oregon Boiler Works, 53
Oregon Historical Society, 163
Ottoman Empire, in World War I, 108, 109–115, 160

P

Page, Matthew, 86
Palestine campaign (World War I), 110, 114, 115
Panama Canal, 56–57, 59
Panic of 1893, 30, 31, 34
"Panzermann" (Boilerplate), 128
Paradox (Russian), 147
"Paris Gun" (German artillery), 118
Parker, Nicholas Stanley, 28
"peaceful penetration" tactics (World War I), 125
Pearl Harbor, attack on, 94
Pershing, John "Black Jack"
    Pancho Villa expedition, 96–97, 101
    Philippine-American War, 79
    Spanish-American War, 70, 96
    World War I, 96, 107, 115–128
Philippine-American War, 68, 74–81, 96, 104
"Philippine insurrection." *See* Philippine-American War
"photo-stories," 64
Pichon, Simone, 84
Pindar (poet), 149–150
Powers, Rich, 146
Proctor, Alexander Phimister, 163
Progressive Era, 30
Pullman Strike of 1894, 35–37
Pullman town (Chicago), 33–36, 162

R

Rankin, Jeanette, 130
Reade, Frank, III, 17
Reade, Frank, Jr., 16, 136, 161
    Archie's letters to, 24, 57, 71, 75, 111
    co-builder of Boilerplate, 16
    Electric Man, 16, 156
    helicopter airships, 86, 158
    Steam Man Mark III, 148, 149, 155, 156
Reade, Frank, Sr., 153–154
Readeworks (robotics company), 156
Real Robots (magazine), 147
"robber barons," 30
"robot," 149
Robot Soldier (toy), 146
Roosevelt, Alice, 95, 131
Roosevelt, Franklin, 64, 131
Roosevelt, Theodore, 42, 96, 160, 161
    and Great White Fleet, 58–62
    and Panama Canal, 56–57, 59
    Philippine-American War, 80
    Rough Riders (Spanish-American War), 68–73, 74, 96, 104, 133, 158, 163
    Russo-Japanese War, 93
    social programs, 129, 131
"Roosevelt's mule," 70, 96, 143
Rosenwald, Julius, 131
Ross, Sir James, 38
Rossum's Universal Robots (R.U.R.) (play), 149
Rough Riders, 68–73, 74, 96, 104, 133, 158, 163
Russia, 83–84, 147
    See also Boxer Rebellion; Russo-Japanese War; World War I
Russo-Japanese War, 61, 87, 88–94, 95, 128

S

Sad Robots (music album), 146, 147
St. Mihiel campaign (World War I), 126
San Francisco Earthquake (1906), 159
San Juan Hill, charge on (Spanish-American War), 66, 70, 72–73, 96, 99, 104, 163
Sankei (company), 146
Schofield, John, 132
Scopes Monkey Trial, 42

Senarens, Luis ("Noname"), 136–137, 156, 157, 161
Seuling, Phil, 144
Shackleton, Ernest, 40
Silverton (cableship), 159
Sino-Japanese War, 83
South Pole expedition, 38–40, 162
Soviet Union, 128, 146
Spain. *See* Philippine-American War; Spanish-American War
Spanish-American War, 62, 66–73, 76–77, 81, 133, 158
    "Buffalo Soldiers" (10th Cavalry), 70, 104–105
    San Juan Hill, charge on, 66, 70, 72–73, 96, 99, 104, 163
    "spheres of influence," 83
"Spring Offensive" (World War I), 117
Square Deal (economic program), 131
"stampeders." *See* "Klondikers"
Star*Reach (Friedrich), 144
Stars (Canadian rock band), 146, 147
Steam Horse (Reade Sr. invention), 154, 155
Steam Man Mark III (Reade Jr. invention), 148, 149, 155, 156
Steam Man of the Prairies, The (Ellis), 153
Steam Men (Reade Sr. inventions), 153–154, 157
Stein, Sarah, 141
Stewart, Robert, 55, 58
Sudan, 45–47
Suez Canal, 45, 59, 108
"suffrage," 130
Suffrage Movement, 26–27, 130, 131

T

Taft, William Howard, 95
"tanks" (World War I), 125
Teddy and his Mechanical Mule (Derwatt), 143
10th Cavalry (U.S. Army). *See* "Buffalo Soldiers" (10th Cavalry)
Tesla, Nikola, 36, 44, 81
    Archie's letters to, 18, 19, 60
    co-builder of Boilerplate, 16
    electromagnetics, 16, 17, 18, 19, 22, 60
Toth, Alex, 145
Trafalgar, Battle of (1805), 92, 106

Treaty of Paris (1898), 74, 81
Treaty of Portsmouth (1905), 93, 95
Treaty of Versailles (1919), 128
Tsiolkovsky, Konstantin, 89
Tsushima Strait, Battle of (1905), 90, 92
"Turk, the" (automaton), 151
Turkey. *See* Ottoman Empire, in World War I
Turner, Frederick Jackson, 30
Twain, Mark, 22, 44, 54, 60, 80, 81
Tzu Hsi (Dowager Empress), 84, 86–87

U

Unexpected Guest, The (film), 139
U.S. Air Force biplane, 99
U.S. Constitution, Nineteenth Amendment to, 27, 130
U.S. Navy. *See* "Great White Fleet"
U.S. Postal Service, 27

V

Vaucanson, Jacques de, 150
Victorian Robot, The (toy), 146
Villa, Pancho, 96–103, 104, 140
Voting Rights Act of 1965, 27

W

War of the Worlds, The (Welles), 131
"War to End All Wars." *See* World War I
"water carriers" (tanks), 125
"Weekend War" (Korean War of 1871), 13
Welles, Orson, 131
Wells, Ida B., 26, 130
"White City" (World's Columbian Exposition), 22, 24, 27, 29, 144
Whitney, Eli, 22
Whittlesey, Charles, 127
Wilson, Woodrow, 96, 116
Wizard of Oz, The (Baum), 27, 29, 31
World Heavyweight Boxing Champion, 62–63
World's Columbian Exposition (1893), 17, 21–30
    "Boilerplate" introduced at, 19, 21–25, 28, 34

Machinery Hall, 22–25, 28, 35
Midway, 25, 27, 138
Palace of Fine Arts, 131, 162
"White City," 22, 24, 27, 29, 144
World's Congress of Representative Women (WCW), 26
World War I, 161
    "Buffalo Soldiers," in, 104
    European theater, 108, 114–128
    Middle Eastern theater, 108–115, 160
    Treaty of Versailles (1919), 128
    Western Front (European Theater), 114–115, 116, 126
World War II, 31, 107, 128
    and collateral damage, 126
    and Germany, 128
    Pearl Harbor, attack on, 94
World Wide Web, 147

Y

"Yank" (U.S. infantryman), 118
Yukon Territory. *See* Klondike Gold Rush
Yup'ik Eskimo, 52, 53

Z

"zoopraxiscope" (motion picture projector), 139

ABOUT THE AUTHORS

Husband-and-wife team Paul Guinan and Anina Bennett have been collaborating in print since 1989. Together they created the groundbreaking science-fiction series *Heartbreakers*. Their 2005 graphic novel, *Heartbreakers Meet Boilerplate*, stars Anina as the main character, and Paul's innovative art was nominated for an Eisner Award. In 1998 they launched their Web site, www.BigRedHair.com.

Paul's eclectic career includes stints as a television personality, cinematographer, commercial illustrator, movie reviewer, production designer, storyboard artist, model maker, and wax-figure restorer for a Ripley's Museum. He produced and hosted the award-winning Chicago cable TV variety show *The Friday Club*, and was lead background artist on the animated series *Stan Lee's Stripperella*. In comics, he has worked on a variety of titles, including cocreating and illustrating *Chronos*, a monthly time-travel series from DC Comics. An avid history buff, Paul has garnered international acclaim as the world's foremost authority on nineteenth-century robots. With Anina at his side, he has lived with the Apache in traditional fashion, sailed the Pacific on a square-rigged brig, and traversed the sands of the Roman Coliseum.

Anina, first published at age fifteen, went on to pen five *Heartbreakers* graphic novels; coauthor *The Art of Comic Book Inking*, now an industry standard; and write reviews, articles, and interviews for various periodicals. As an editor, she's worked on everything from *Star Wars* to Supreme Court briefs. Anina's career has taken her from Chicago, where she cut her teeth at First Comics; to Dark Horse Comics in Oregon, where she collaborated with renowned author Harlan Ellison; to Denmark, where she handled Mickey Mouse tales for multimedia giant Egmont. Anina is a founding board member of Friends of Lulu, a nonprofit organization that works to get more women involved in comics. She has served as both a judge and a presenter for the Eisner Awards, and has taught comics-writing workshops for students of all ages.

Paul and Anina were raised in Chicago and have known each other for an astoundingly long time. They now reside in Portland, Oregon, with their Weimaraner, Sisko.

BOILERPLATE

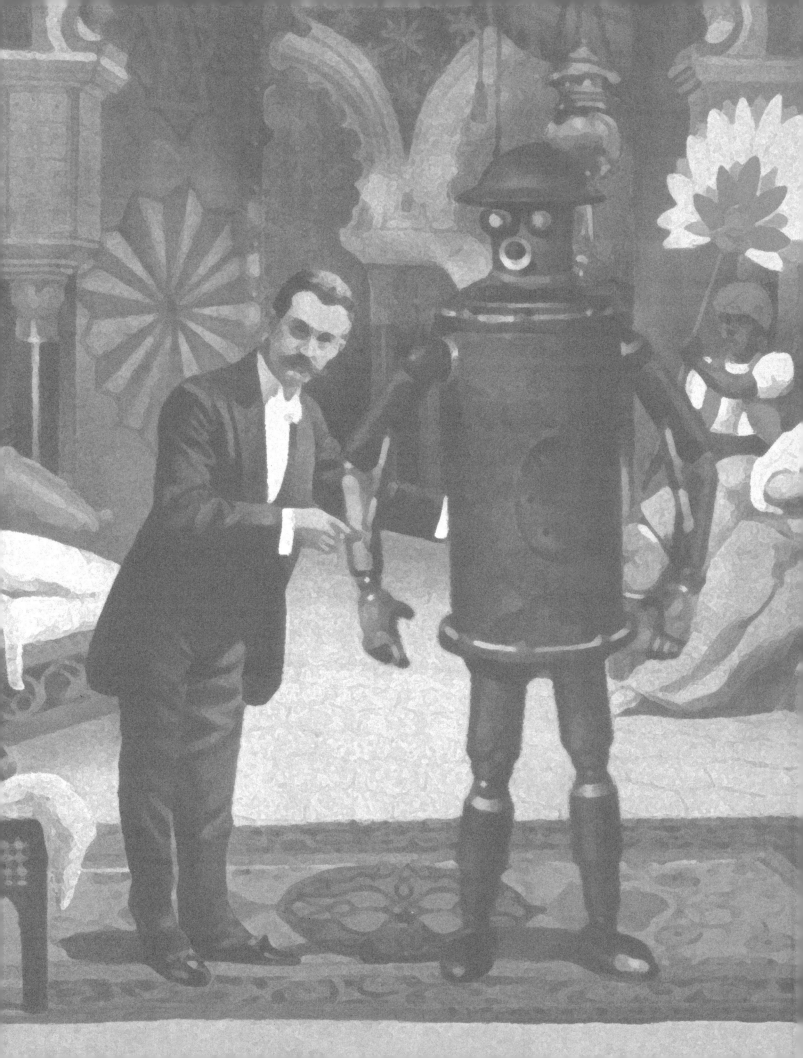